Paws & Peace

Heartwarming Bedtime Stories for Women and Their Dogs

Molly Harris

Contents

Introduction

There's a kind of peace that only comes when a dog curls up beside you. You know the one. When your shoulders finally drop, your breathing slows, and there's nothing to prove or perform. Just presence. Just love. Just the quiet comfort of knowing you're not alone.

This book was made for that feeling.

Paws & Peace is a collection of gentle bedtime stories for women who love their dogs deeply... like family, like home, like something sacred. It's for the woman who talks to her dog more honestly than most people. Who cries into fur. Who finds calm in the rhythm of walks, the warmth of a curled-up body, and the silent language that only the two of you speak.

These stories are soft on purpose. There are no sharp turns here. No deadlines or drama. Just simple moments: a shared glance, a stretch on the living room rug, a memory that floats up while the kettle hums. Each one is a small invitation to rest and to remember that love, especially the kind that trots beside you on four paws, can be the gentlest anchor.

You can read one story or many. You can read with your dog snoring beside you, or with her leash waiting by the door. There are no rules here. Only calm.

So settle in. Exhale. Let the day go.

Your dog is here. And so are you. And for now, that is more than enough.

Chapter 1

The First Tail Wag

She didn't mean to cry over the slipper.

It was just a fuzzy, half-flattened thing tucked under the edge of the bed, right where her foot always found it. But tonight, the light caught it differently, tilted sideways from the hallway lamp, and she saw the frayed edge at the toe. The bite marks. Tiny ones. Like a secret signature from long ago.

She sat down slowly on the edge of the bed, slipper in hand, and exhaled through her nose. One of those deep, quiet sighs that carried more than breath. That slipper had no real monetary value. No sentimental inscription. No grand story attached.

Except it did. At least to her.

"Do you remember this?" she asked softly, turning her head toward the bundle of fur already curled in her usual spot. Luna didn't lift her head. She only gave a sleepy shift of paws and a deeper sigh, settling into the blankets like they were clouds she'd claimed as her own.

Of course Luna remembered. The chewed slipper was just the beginning.

That first day had been chaos and softness and something that felt suspiciously like falling in love.

Luna had cried the whole ride home. Sharp little yelps from the crate in the passenger seat, even though she had her favorite flannel blanket tucked in beside her. The sound pierced through the music and the soft reassurances she kept whispering, words that tumbled out without planning: lullabies, nonsense, promises.

"You're okay," she had whispered between traffic lights. "You're not alone. I've got you."

She wasn't sure which one of them needed to hear it more.

When they pulled into the driveway of her apartment building, the rain started. Not a downpour, just a light mist. Like the sky wasn't ready to cry full tears yet but needed to say something.

She opened the passenger door and crouched down beside the crate. "Well," she said, unlocking it, "this is it. We live here now. Together."

Luna tumbled out. Legs too long, paws too big, ears flopping into her eyes, and promptly peed on the rug in the hallway.

That was their first official moment as roommates.

She smiled now, rubbing her thumb over the slipper's worn fabric. Those tiny indents left by puppy teeth weren't damage; they were proof of something beginning.

Across the bed, Luna stretched. Older now. Slower. Her muzzle was dusted with gray, her eyes cloudier in the right light. But the weight of her in the room was the same, steady and grounding, like a lighthouse beam that kept her from drifting too far from shore.

She leaned toward the lamp to switch it off, but her hand paused midair.

Not yet. She wasn't ready to let the night take over. Not until the memory finished saying what it needed to.

The first night had been... difficult.

She had read all the blogs and books. Set up the crate with a soft towel and a ticking clock to mimic a heartbeat. But Luna whimpered endlessly, a sad, panicked sound that tugged at every nerve in her body.

She tried soothing words. A hot water bottle. Her own worn T-shirt. Nothing worked.

Eventually, she laid on the hardwood floor beside the crate, one hand laced through the metal bars, whispering, "It's okay. You're safe now," like a mantra.

Around 2 a.m., she gave up. Cracked open the crate, lifted Luna into her arms, and curled up in bed.

"Just this once," she'd told herself.

It became every night after that.

The first tail wag had come the next morning. She remembered it so clearly.

Still in her pajamas, clutching her coffee like a lifeline, she sat on the kitchen floor with Luna curled nearby. She'd offered a tiny piece of banana, hoping the pup wouldn't snub it. Luna sniffed suspiciously, licked her hand once, and then, just once, wagged her tail.

A soft thump against the tile floor.

That little movement said more than words could.

It was the first yes.

Yes to her voice. Yes to her presence. Yes to the idea that maybe, just maybe, this odd arrangement could work.

The bond rooted quietly, like ivy under a windowsill, unnoticed at first but growing stronger each day.

She glanced now at the digital clock beside the bed—10:42. The book she'd meant to finish sat face-down on the nightstand. She picked it up, thumbed through a few pages, then let it fall back with a soft thud.

Some nights, stories helped her drift. But tonight, the one already unfolding in her mind was gentler than anything bound between pages.

Luna let out a little huff in her sleep. Her legs twitched, chasing dream rabbits, most likely.

She reached across the bed and rested her hand on Luna's back. That familiar curve, the rise and fall of breath, the warmth that never failed to soothe.

Another memory crept in.

That first week had been soaked in rain. Constant drizzle, puddles blooming like pop-up lakes on sidewalks, towels hanging off every doorknob. Every outing meant a wet, squirming puppy and mud-speckled jeans.

By the third bath, they both looked like creatures from a swamp.

Afterward, she wrapped Luna in a towel and collapsed on the couch. Luna climbed up without hesitation, curled into a tiny cinnamon roll of fur on her chest, and fell asleep. Damp, shivering, but finally quiet.

She remembered lying there, watching the rain drip down the window and whispering, "You're home."

And knowing. Truly knowing it was true.

That was the first time Luna fell asleep on her chest.

It was far from the last.

She shifted slightly now, easing back onto her pillow. Luna responded, stretching one paw until it rested gently against her ankle. Even asleep, she always knew where she was.

Another moment surfaced. Not a big one. Just an ordinary Tuesday a few years back.

She'd come home late from work, tired and frayed. Her boss had snapped at her, she'd spilled coffee down her shirt, and the train had stalled underground for twenty minutes. She wanted nothing more than to scream into a pillow.

But when she opened the door, Luna was there. Sitting. Waiting. Tail tapping.

That tail thump. The slow, steady beat had melted something in her. She knelt, face to fur, and whispered, "Thank you."

They didn't go for a walk that night. Instead, they sat on the floor, back pressed to the cabinets, sharing a bag of popcorn and the comfort of just being.

The slipper slipped from her lap and landed with a soft thud. She didn't bother to pick it up. It belonged there.

She turned off the lamp. Darkness settled around her like a familiar blanket.

But the memories still flickered.

There was the time Luna got sick. Nothing serious, but enough to send a jolt of panic through her. The vet was reassuring, the medicine worked quickly, but those few days of worry had carved a new depth into their bond. She'd sat on the bathroom floor at 2 a.m., stroking Luna's ears, whispering stories until they both dozed off beside the water bowl.

And then there was the mountain trip. The cabin with creaky floors and the fireplace that barely worked. Luna had spent the entire first evening trying to catch falling snow through the window. She'd laughed until her sides hurt.

Or the time Luna had barked furiously at a paper bag on the porch for five minutes straight, convinced it was a threat to the household. Brave, ridiculous, utterly herself.

So many days. So many moments.

Little ones, mostly.

But that's what a life is, isn't it? Not grand milestones. Not the big events or perfect pictures. Just a thousand tiny threads woven together.

Luna had been there for all of them.

The heartbreaks. The career changes. The birthdays spent alone and the holidays filled with noise. The morning jogs and the midnight snacks. The new apartments and the sad goodbyes.

Through it all: tail wags. Soft ears. Quiet company.

The thing about dogs, what they give, isn't just loyalty. It's presence. Unfiltered, uncomplicated presence. A kind of love that doesn't waver. Doesn't need words.

Just warmth. And waiting. And the thump of a tail that says, "You're not alone."

She curled onto her side, finally letting her body melt into the mattress.

Luna stirred, shifting in sleep until they were back-to-back.

Still. Even now. Like puzzle pieces that had never needed adjusting.

She let her eyes close.

But she held onto the sound of that first tail thump.

That small, perfect yes.

The beginning of everything.

Chapter 2

Not My Dog (Until She Was)

The email said two weeks. That was the deal.

Just a short-term foster until the rescue could find her a proper home. One with a yard, maybe kids, someone more "dog person-ish" than Claire. The kind of person who didn't hesitate. The kind who kept treats in their coat pockets and had lint rollers in every room because dog hair was just part of life.

That wasn't Claire.

She had agreed because her friend at the shelter sounded desperate, and because saying no felt too heavy that day. It had been a hard week, full of missed deadlines, weird silences, and a lingering sadness she couldn't quite name. So she said yes.

Just two weeks.

The dog arrived on a Tuesday afternoon.

She came with a small crate, a bright orange leash, and a name that didn't seem to suit her: Peaches. As in, "She's a total peach!" Except this dog was not. She was timid, wiry, and had the nervous energy of a squirrel in traffic. Her ribs showed under patchy white fur, and her eyes, huge and amber and always scanning, never stopped moving.

"She's sweet once she warms up," her friend promised, handing over a bag of kibble and a hopeful smile. "Just be patient."

Claire stood in the entryway after the door closed, Peaches crouched behind her legs, and thought, What have I done?

She hadn't prepped for this. No dog bed. No toys. She'd tossed an old towel on the living room rug and filled a bowl with water. She hadn't expected much.

Peaches hadn't either.

For the first two days, the dog barely moved from her corner under the table. She ate only when the room was empty and flinched at the sound of the fridge opening. She didn't bark. She didn't beg. She just existed like a shadow.

"This is temporary," Claire reminded herself aloud, sipping tea on the couch while watching the shape of the dog barely visible in the dim light. "Just two weeks."

By the fourth night, something shifted.

She had been working late, tapping away on her laptop while half-listening to the hum of the heater. At some point, she noticed the silence had changed. It had texture now. Breath, weight, presence.

She glanced down.

Peaches was lying at her feet.

Not under the table. Not behind the chair. At her feet.

Staring up at her like she'd been there all along.

Claire didn't say anything. Didn't reach down to pet her. Just let the moment hang in the quiet. A truce.

That weekend, they went for a walk.

It was clumsy at first. Peaches didn't seem to understand the leash, and every passing car sent her sideways. But they made it to the corner and back. Then, the next day, around the block. On Sunday, they went all the way to the park.

Peaches walked a little taller coming home.

She started following Claire from room to room after that. Still no barking. No sudden affection. But she'd quietly appear, by the bathroom door, beside the couch, even outside the shower, curled like a comma on the mat.

The towel on the rug was replaced with a small dog bed. Claire ordered it late one night without thinking too hard about it.

"This isn't your home," she said gently as she placed it down. "But you can get comfortable while you're here."

Peaches sniffed it, turned three tight circles, and laid down with a sigh.

On day twelve, the rescue called.

"We think we have a match! Family with a backyard and another dog. They'd love to meet her."

Claire stared at the phone a beat too long.

"Oh," she said finally. "That's... great."

She hung up and turned around. Peaches was sitting at the top of the stairs, head tilted, waiting.

Claire made pasta that night. Burned the garlic. Forgot to salt the water. She kept glancing down as she stirred the sauce, waiting for the usual shape curled behind her to appear.

But Peaches didn't come to the kitchen.

She was in the living room. In her bed. Waiting.

The morning of the meet-and-greet, Claire didn't say anything. Not to the dog. Not to herself.

She moved quietly, packing up the orange leash, folding the towel, placing the nearly full bag of kibble into a paper bag. Peaches sat by the door, as if she knew something was shifting.

She wasn't wagging.

She never really wagged.

The tail would twitch occasionally, or sway like a metronome when she was half-asleep and dreaming. But she never wagged full out, like dogs in cartoons or the park or in stories where they just knew they were loved.

Claire checked her phone. The family was running late.

She glanced at Peaches. "Want to go for a ride?"

The ears perked just slightly. Not enough to be excited. Just enough to say: I hear you.

The drive was quiet. A short one. Only fifteen minutes, but it felt longer. The road curved through neighborhoods Claire barely noticed, houses with wreaths still hanging in the windows even though Christmas had passed weeks ago.

Peaches stared out the passenger window.

Claire parked in front of the rescue's side gate, turned off the engine, and sat still for a moment.

She reached over, hand hovering just above the dog's fur.

"Listen," she said quietly. "This isn't goodbye. Not really. You're going to be okay. You'll have space to run and another dog to—"

Peaches looked at her then. Not just a glance. A full, direct look. Soft. Still. Patient.

Claire didn't finish the sentence.

Instead, she took a breath and opened the door.

The woman from the rescue greeted them with a warm smile and gentle hands. She crouched low and called Peaches' name in a bright voice that didn't quite match the softness of the morning.

Peaches didn't move.

"That's okay," the woman said. "It happens. Sometimes they're nervous. It's a big transition."

She reached out slowly, offering a hand. Peaches blinked but didn't lean forward.

"Why don't you wait in the play yard?" the woman offered. "The family should be here any minute. We can give them some time to warm up to each other."

Claire nodded and led Peaches through the gate.

The play yard was mostly gravel, a few scattered toys, a weathered bench under the skeleton of a maple tree. Claire sat. Peaches lay down by her feet.

Ten minutes passed. Then fifteen.

The wind picked up. Gray clouds gathered over the fence. Claire watched a leaf tumble across the stones and glanced at the time.

Then she heard the woman's voice through the intercom.

"The family had to reschedule. The daughter woke up with a fever. I'm so sorry."

Claire looked down. Peaches hadn't moved.

The rescue staff offered to keep her there until the next meet-up. "To avoid more back-and-forth," they said.

But something clenched inside Claire at the thought. A quiet twist.

"It's okay," she said. "I'll take her home. It's only a few more days."

They didn't talk about it on the way back.

Claire didn't speak, and Peaches didn't stare out the window this time. She curled into the seat and closed her eyes.

By the time they pulled into the driveway, light rain had started to fall.

Claire opened the door, letting Peaches trot in first. The house smelled like laundry and cinnamon from the candle she'd left burning too long.

Peaches did her usual lap. Hallway, couch, water bowl, and then climbed into her bed.

Later that night, Claire sat on the couch, legs tucked underneath her, a book in her lap she didn't really read.

Peaches lay just inches away, ears twitching at every creak of the house.

She glanced down. Watched the dog breathe.

"This wasn't supposed to matter so much," she whispered.

But of course, it did.

The next day, they walked longer than usual.

It was early, just after sunrise. The neighborhood still felt wrapped in sleep, the air soft and cold against Claire's cheeks. Peaches moved slowly at first, then picked up speed as they reached the corner.

They turned down the street with the tall pine trees. The one that smelled like sap and always had squirrels darting just out of reach. Peaches perked up. She didn't chase. Just watched. Curious.

At the end of the block, there was a bench Claire rarely stopped at. But today, she did.

She sat.

Peaches sat, too.

The sky was still pink in places, and the world had that hush it only gets when it's just beginning.

Claire reached out and placed a hand gently on Peaches' back.

Warm. Steady.

Still hers.

At least for now.

The second family never called back.

"Things changed," the rescue explained. "It happens."

Claire didn't ask for more details.

By the end of the second week, there was no third family lined up.

The rescue checked in politely, promised they were "actively looking," and thanked her again for "being so patient."

But inside her inbox, there was silence.

And inside her house, there was Peaches.

She stopped telling people she was "just fostering."

Not on purpose. Not with a grand announcement. It just faded from the way she spoke about Peaches.

At the coffee shop, when someone asked, "What kind of dog is she?" Claire said, "Not sure. Maybe a terrier mix."

At the vet, when the receptionist asked, "And this is your dog?" she replied, "Yes. Peaches. She's here for her boosters."

At home, when she spoke to her in the way people do when no one else is around, she no longer said, "You're not staying," but, "Come here, silly girl," and, "Dinner's ready," and, "Let's go home," even though they were already there.

It wasn't one decision. It was a thousand tiny ones.

Like how she rearranged the living room so Peaches could see out the window from her bed.

Or how she moved her morning meetings back fifteen minutes so they could take their walk while the street was still quiet.

Or how she started sleeping on the side of the bed that creaked less when she got up in the night, so she wouldn't disturb her.

She bought her a proper tag. Pewter, with her name etched on one side and her phone number on the other. The sound of it tapping against her collar became part of the soundtrack of her life.

The email from the rescue came a week later. A polite subject line: "New Potential Match for Peaches!"

Claire read it three times before closing her laptop.

And then she just sat there.

It was late. Rain again. The house smelled like chamomile tea and damp socks.

Peaches was lying by the couch, chin resting on her front paws, eyes half-closed.

Claire watched her breathe. Watched her chest rise and fall, soft and slow.

"This was never the plan," she said aloud. "I'm not a dog person."

Peaches didn't stir.

"But I think you're mine."

The words felt too big and too small at the same time.

She didn't send a reply to the rescue that night. Or the next.

She meant to.

She even opened the message a few times, hovering over the keyboard with fingers that couldn't quite type the words.

But every time she thought about someone else clipping on that orange leash...

Someone else walking her down the street with the tall pines...

Someone else sitting with her on the bench in the early morning hush...

She closed the laptop again.

She told the rescue two days later.

Called them instead of writing, because that felt more human.

There was a brief silence on the other end after she said the words, "I'd like to adopt her."

Then her friend laughed—gentle, not teasing.

"I was wondering when you'd admit that," she said.

They handled the paperwork quickly. Efficiently. Claire barely remembered the details.

But she remembered taking the final signature to the mailbox.

She remembered the cold air and the way Peaches walked beside her. Not pulling, not trailing, just walking in rhythm like she always had.

On the way back, she stopped at the little pet store on the corner.

She bought a new collar. Dark blue. Soft. Sturdy.

She held it in her hands before putting it on her. Running her thumbs over the stitching, like it was a vow she hadn't realized she was making.

Peaches sniffed it once and then leaned into her, still and calm.

Claire clipped it on.

The tag jingled just the same, but everything felt different.

They settled into something real after that.

Not perfect. Not magical. Just real.

Peaches never did like toys much. She'd pick one up, mouth it once or twice, then drop it like it had offended her.

She hated baths. Tolerated the vet. Refused to eat anything that smelled remotely like sweet potato.

But she loved the couch on rainy afternoons. Loved the narrow patch of sun that stretched across the bedroom floor each morning. Loved, quietly and completely, Claire, the woman who had once insisted she wasn't hers.

She wagged now.

Not wildly. Not the cartoon kind of wag. But enough.

Enough to say: "I'm home. I know it. I feel it."

And sometimes, when she dreamed, her paws would twitch and her tail would thump against the dog bed.

One soft beat at a time.

One night, almost a year later, Claire was curled in bed reading when Peaches stood up suddenly from her spot near the door.

She padded over, slow and purposeful, then jumped gently onto the bed.

That was new.

Claire had never invited her up. Had never discouraged her, but Peaches had always seemed content nearby.

But tonight, she climbed onto the quilt, turned three deliberate circles, and curled up in the crook of Claire's knees.

Claire didn't move.

She just placed her hand over Peaches' back, feeling the steady rhythm of breath under her palm.

The book slipped from her lap to the floor, forgotten.

Outside, the wind nudged the windows.

Inside, the house was warm.

"I'm glad you're here," Claire whispered, not sure if she was speaking to the dog or to the life that had quietly bloomed around her.

Peaches let out a long, slow sigh. The kind that comes only when a body feels completely safe.

And with that, they both drifted toward sleep.

Claire would think about that night often.

Not because it was extraordinary. But because it was quiet.

And because quiet moments, she'd come to learn, were the ones that lasted longest.

Not my dog.

Until she was.

And thank goodness for that.

Chapter 3

The Sock Thief

Josie had always considered herself a reasonably tidy person. Not obsessively neat, not the label-maker kind, but organized enough to know where her favorite socks were.

Until Roo.

Roo was a Border Collie mix with bright eyes, boundless energy, and a habit of looking deeply guilty right before doing something very bold. Josie had adopted her at seven months old from a local rescue, charmed by her lopsided ears and the way she tilted her head like she was asking, *Are you sure you're ready for this?*

She hadn't been. Not really.

But Roo had brought life and light into the quiet house that had, up until then, been mostly filled with Josie's books, plants, and the soft hum of a tea kettle.

The socks started disappearing about a month in.

The first time, Josie blamed herself. She had done laundry the night before and must've dropped one.

The second time, she frowned. "I swear I had a matching pair."

The third time, Roo was sitting suspiciously still beside the laundry basket with her tail wrapped neatly around one paw.

Josie crouched. "Roo…"

Roo wagged. Just once. The soft, stealthy kind.

And that's when Josie knew.

She pulled the laundry basket aside and found—nothing.

"No way," she muttered. "Did you eat it?"

Roo trotted to the couch and flopped down with an exaggerated yawn.

The mystery deepened.

The next morning, Josie opened her sock drawer and, sure enough, one sock was missing again. Same basket. Same setup. Same innocent-looking dog.

"Okay," she said, pulling her hair into a messy bun. "You want to play detective? Let's play."

She spent the better part of an hour crawling around the house on her hands and knees, checking under furniture, behind pillows, even inside her boots.

Nothing.

Roo followed, tail wagging like it was all a game.

That afternoon, while vacuuming behind the couch, Josie

bumped something soft. She reached down, lifted the corner of the slipcover, and froze.

There, in a tidy little nest, were five socks.

Not chewed. Not shredded.

Just... borrowed.

Josie stared at Roo, who peeked around the doorway with a look that said, *Oh. You found it.*

"You're a collector," Josie whispered. "A soft goods bandit."

Roo padded in and, with all the elegance of a practiced thief, dropped a sixth sock onto the pile and sat down proudly.

From that day on, it became a thing.

Every night, Josie would drop a clean sock, just one, on the edge of the laundry basket. And every morning, it would be gone.

She never said a word. She didn't need to.

Roo carried out her mission with quiet consistency, always placing the sock neatly in her secret stash beneath the couch.

On Sunday mornings, Josie would gently lift the slipcover, peek at the pile, and whisper, "Seven. Good job."

It wasn't just about socks anymore.

It became a kind of comfort. A sign that things were steady. That each day, Roo did something small and strange and beautiful just because it felt right.

One Saturday evening, Josie had a bad day. Nothing dramatic. Just the usual swirl of too many things: late work emails, an overcooked dinner, a dropped jar of jam that left a sticky mess on the kitchen floor.

She sighed and sank onto the couch, rubbing her temples.

Roo jumped up beside her and placed something gently in her lap.

A sock.

A small, rolled-up, lavender sock that had once belonged to a pair Josie wore on rainy days.

She looked down at it, then up at Roo.

And something inside her softened.

"You're too good," she whispered. "Way too good."

She placed the sock on the armrest and rested her hand on Roo's back. They sat there for a long time, just breathing.

One morning, Josie woke late. Her alarm hadn't gone off. Her meeting was in fifteen minutes, and she still hadn't fed Roo or found her lucky socks.

"Chaos," she muttered, yanking open drawers and tugging on yesterday's jeans.

Roo barked once, not frantic, but pointed.

Josie glanced at her. "I know, I know. I'm running behind."

Roo wagged and trotted to the couch.

Josie paused.

Then followed.

Roo nosed the slipcover aside and backed up.

Inside was not just the usual pile, but a brand-new sock. One Josie had never seen before.

Pink. Fuzzy. With little white stars stitched near the cuff.

Josie crouched and picked it up, puzzled.

"Where did you get this?"

Roo did a slow spin and sat down.

It took her a minute, but then she remembered: her neighbor's teenage daughter had dropped her gym bag on their shared porch step the day before. Roo had been out in the yard at the time.

Josie shook her head. "You're expanding your operation."

She returned the sock later that afternoon after rinsing it and adding a note: *Sorry. Roo has a thing for socks. She means well.*

The neighbor laughed and wrote back, *Honestly, same. She's welcome to borrow anytime.*

That night, Josie added a fresh sock to the laundry basket, placing it like an offering.

"Just ours," she said with a smile. "Let's not get the whole block involved."

Roo blinked slowly, tail swishing once.

Message received.

Months passed.

The routine remained.

Sometimes Roo skipped a day. Sometimes she brought back an

old favorite, one Josie had forgotten even existed. Once, she brought two, when Josie had had an especially long week.

The stash under the couch grew and shrank with the rhythm of their days. On quiet mornings, Josie would peek in and feel a little jolt of gratitude for this small, strange tradition that belonged only to them.

No one else would understand.

But she didn't need them to.

Because Roo did.

One sock at a time.

Chapter 4

The Morning Stretch Match

Marian didn't need an alarm clock anymore.

Not since retirement.

Not since Jasper.

He had a way of knowing when the sun was about to rise. Always just a few minutes before it painted the walls of her bedroom in soft gold. No barking, no chaos. Just a quiet rhythm of toenails clicking on the hallway floor, then the unmistakable sound of a sigh as he settled beside her bed. Waiting.

Marian would open one eye. Jasper would thump his tail against the carpet. Then she'd smile.

"Five more minutes, boy," she'd murmur, already reaching for her slippers.

But they both knew it would be less than two.

She didn't like to waste the morning.

Especially not with Jasper.

He was an Australian Shepherd with stormy gray fur and a habit of tilting his head at nearly everything she said. "Time to stretch?" would get a tail wag. "Coffee first," would earn a huff. But "Yoga mat?" That was the magic phrase.

Because Jasper, as it turned out, was not just a herding dog.

He was a stretching dog.

It had started as a joke.

The day after she brought him home from the rescue, newly retired and slightly unsure of what to do with herself, she had unrolled her old blue yoga mat in the living room, intent on loosening the creaks in her back.

Jasper had watched from the couch, head tilted, eyes bright. Then, as Marian bent forward into a wide-legged stretch, he slid off the cushions and flopped onto the mat beside her.

"Don't mind me," she said, half laughing.

But when she arched into a cat-cow stretch, Jasper did too. His front legs down, rear in the air, tail wagging like it had a metronome.

Marian blinked.

"Did you just... down-dog a down dog?"

He barked once. Just once. As if to say: Obviously.

And that was the beginning.

Now, every morning began with the same routine. She'd unroll the mat, now slightly frayed at the edges, and Jasper would trot over, his nails ticking softly against the hardwood floor. He'd wait until she was in her first forward fold, and then he'd join her. Always.

They didn't move in perfect harmony. Marian's joints had their own ideas. Jasper liked to insert a play bow into nearly every pose. But the rhythm they shared was theirs alone. Quiet. Fluid. Grounding.

It had become their match, breath for breath and stretch for stretch. A gentle way of greeting the day together.

This morning, as Marian opened the back door to let in the breeze, Jasper bounded ahead and sat near the patio, sniffing the new air like a sommelier tasting wine.

The garden was just beginning to bloom, with lavender, rosemary, and tiny clusters of white blossoms on the edge of the fence. Marian stood barefoot in the doorway, letting the cool air touch her face. The mat waited inside, already rolled out in its usual spot between the bookshelves and the piano she hadn't touched in years.

She looked down at Jasper.

"Shall we?"

He turned immediately and trotted back in, tail high.

She started with her usual deep breath, arms raised to the ceiling.

Jasper stretched forward, front paws down, back arched just enough to call it coordinated.

"Nice form," she told him.

They moved through their slow sequence: shoulder rolls, neck circles, long pauses in child's pose. Jasper sprawled beside her, occasionally nuzzling her hand as if to remind her she wasn't doing it alone.

This was what Marian hadn't known she needed after retirement. Not just the freedom, not just the quiet, but the rhythm of something shared.

Before Jasper, mornings had felt aimless. Too quiet. Too slow.

She'd make tea, check the news, fold a dish towel that didn't really need folding.

It had been only six weeks between her farewell luncheon at the library and the day she visited the rescue "just to look."

Jasper had been in the last kennel.

Curled tight, wary-eyed, coat too long around his ears.

She'd stood there for nearly ten minutes before kneeling.

"You've got secrets, don't you?" she'd whispered.

He hadn't moved, not at first.

But then, slowly, he stood.

Walked to the gate.

Sat down.

And placed one paw against the bars.

The staff told her later that he didn't do that for anyone else.

Marian had just nodded. She didn't have words for the feeling.

It was like someone had exhaled a breath she hadn't known she was holding.

So she brought him home.

And learned quickly that he didn't like thunder, didn't care for peanut butter, and absolutely despised car washes. But he loved early mornings, lying under the dining table while she read, and being close to her. Always close.

Especially when she stretched.

Now, with both of them on the mat, Marian reached for her toes and let her breath settle into a slow, familiar rhythm.

"You know," she said between stretches, "we're probably not the most graceful yoga duo."

Jasper yawned dramatically.

"But we've got commitment. That counts for something."

Outside, a bird chirped. A lawn mower buzzed faintly in the distance.

Inside, the room held its gentle quiet, filled only by the sound of Marian's breath and Jasper's tail tapping once, twice, against the mat.

She stayed in her final pose longer than usual, legs crossed, eyes closed, hands resting softly on her knees.

Jasper lay beside her, head on her foot.

They didn't need music.

Didn't need mirrors or goals or names for every pose.

They just needed this.

A shared ritual.

A beginning.

By mid-morning, the sun had stretched itself wide across the backyard.

Marian stood by the sink, rinsing blueberries into a small bowl while Jasper lounged just outside the sliding glass door, chin on his paws, eyes half-closed. His fur glowed in the light, and for a second, he looked like a painting, something oil-brushed and timeless.

She carried the bowl out to the patio and sat on the old wicker bench. Jasper stirred, but didn't rise. He knew the routine: stretches, then fruit, then a slow wander through the yard before the day truly began.

It had taken Marian a while to admit how much she liked the structure of it.

She wasn't used to being unneeded.

Forty-two years in the public library system had given her plenty to do. There had always been a storytime, a shelving project, a student researching something obscure and wonderful. She had loved the quiet busyness of it all. The hum of fluorescent lights, the smell of old pages, the way regular patrons knew her by name.

And then, one day, it ended.

Cake in the breakroom. A card signed by everyone. A gift card to the garden center.

And then... nothing.

At first, she pretended it was fine. That retirement was rest, freedom, breathing room.

But deep down, she missed the rhythm. The being expected.

Until Jasper gave it back.

In a different form, yes, but no less grounding.

Now she had mornings that mattered. A living being who noticed when she showed up. A wagging tail that said: I see you.

After her blueberries, Marian stood and stretched once more, not the full routine, just a soft reach toward the sky, then a gentle forward fold. Jasper joined her without being asked, doing his customary bow and low groan as if he'd been waiting for that exact moment.

They walked the garden path after that, Marian pointing out blooms as if he were a fellow gardener.

"Lavender's holding on longer this year," she said.

Jasper sniffed it. Sneezed.

"I know, I know. It's strong."

They passed the rosemary bush, the cracked birdbath, the small fig tree she'd rescued from a clearance sale last fall.

Every step slow. Shared.

Later that week, a new neighbor saw them stretching in the yard and waved over the fence.

"That your yoga coach?" she called, nodding toward Jasper.

Marian laughed. "He's strict. But fair."

"I love it," the woman said. "You do this every day?"

"Every morning," Marian replied. "Rain or shine."

She didn't add that on rainy days, they simply moved the mat to the hallway. That sometimes she lit a candle and let the scent of eucalyptus fill the house while they both breathed in tandem.

It wasn't for show.

It was for them.

The neighbor, Cynthia, she'd said her name was, began waving more often. Asking about Jasper. Offering fresh basil from her windowsill planter. One morning, she even brought over an extra yoga mat, rolled in a ribbon.

"In case your assistant wants his own," she said with a wink.

Marian thanked her, set it next to hers, and Jasper immediately claimed it, stretching out like royalty on a new throne.

They laughed.

Cynthia didn't stay long, but Marian felt lighter after she left.

It was funny how rituals, even small ones, invited people in.

The next week, Jasper injured his paw.

Not badly, just a tender pad, likely from something sharp along the walking trail. But it kept him off the mat for two mornings. He watched from the couch, ears slightly drooped, as Marian stretched alone.

"It's not the same without you," she told him.

He blinked, as if to say: I know.

On the third day, when she unrolled the mat, Jasper limped slowly over and laid beside her, not stretching, not moving, just being close.

She adjusted her poses to stay low, near the floor. Rested her hand on his back during savasana.

When the session ended, she stayed there, fingers buried in his fur.

It didn't matter what they did, she realized.

Only that they did it together.

The weather turned cooler that week, just enough for Marian to start wearing socks in the mornings again.

She'd always loved the fall, its quiet invitation to slow down, its rust-colored honesty. But this year, it brought something else too: a memory that slipped in alongside the wind.

It was a photograph, tucked into the back of a drawer she'd been cleaning in a moment of ambition.

Her and Caroline.

Laughing, sun-soaked, barefoot on the beach with yoga mats slung over their shoulders and a coffee cart in the background. It had to be twenty years ago. Maybe more.

Caroline had been her best friend since college. The kind of friend you shared rooms and recipes and heartbreak with. The kind who knew when to talk and when to just sit beside you, saying nothing at all.

They'd done yoga together every Thursday night back when they were both still working, laughing through clumsy poses, whispering during savasana, promising they'd keep doing it until they were old and gray.

But things changed.

Caroline moved to the coast to care for her sister.

Marian stayed.

They texted. Called. Wrote letters, even.

But the mat stayed rolled up for years after that.

Until Jasper.

Marian sat with the photo in her lap, her thumb brushing over the crease that ran across Caroline's smile.

She didn't cry.

But she didn't move for a long time, either.

The next morning, her stretches were slower. Softer.

She didn't speak much or offer Jasper his usual commentary. She just moved carefully and quietly, as if she were listening for something under the surface.

Jasper stayed close, his body brushing hers during each pose.

She moved into a seated twist, and he mirrored her with a long stretch to the left, then the right. Marian smiled, even if it didn't quite reach her eyes.

"You're good for me, you know that?"

Jasper rested his head on her knee.

Later, she took the photo and slipped it into the corner of the hallway mirror. Not to forget. Just to remember better.

That night, she lit a candle and stretched again, alone this time, just before bed.

Jasper stayed nearby, watching.

At the end, when she lay on her back with her hands over her heart, she whispered, "Thanks, Caroline."

And somewhere in the quiet of her body, she felt the echo of two women on a beach, promising they'd never stop moving forward.

That Saturday, the neighborhood kids were out early, shouting and riding bikes down the street. Jasper stood at the window, tail wagging with interest but no urgency.

"Not your crew," Marian said, sipping her tea.

Jasper didn't move from his post.

The morning felt too nice to stay inside, so Marian carried the mat out to the patio. The sun was warm enough, and the sound of leaves rustling overhead was its own kind of music. They moved together under the open sky, Jasper rolling onto his back at one point, paws curled, tongue lolling to the side.

"Show off," she murmured.

He rolled back up and gave her his best down dog. She laughed, the sound lifting into the branches above them.

It wasn't about the stretches anymore. It hadn't been for a while. It was about presence. Being here. Fully.

They finished their practice with Jasper curled on one end of the mat and Marian lying beside him, palms open to the sky, eyes closed.

The breeze tickled the edge of her sleeve. Somewhere across the street, a wind chime began to sing.

She stayed like that for a while, longer than usual. Not because she was waiting for anything, but because nothing else was pulling her away.

Eventually, Jasper shifted and rested his head against her arm. Marian turned toward him and smiled.

"Ready to start the day?" she asked.

He didn't answer, of course. Just blinked and wagged his tail.

And that was the only yes she needed.

Chapter 5

The Sunday Pancake Pact

The first pancake was an accident.

Tessa hadn't even meant to make breakfast that morning. It was a Sunday in late October, gray and drizzly, the kind of day that pressed softly on your shoulders and made everything feel slower. She had planned to just have coffee and a banana. Maybe scroll through her phone. Maybe not.

But Maple had other ideas.

The golden doodle, barely a year old then, bounded into the kitchen with her usual mix of excitement and chaos, skidding slightly on the tile as she rounded the corner. She sat squarely in front of the pantry, tail thumping the floor with gentle insistence.

"What?" Tessa asked, lifting her coffee to her lips. "We already did breakfast. You ate."

Maple tilted her head.

"You don't even like bananas."

Another tail thump.

Tessa sighed, set the mug down, and turned toward the cabinet.

Pancakes. Why not?

She hadn't made them in ages. Not since… well. Not since things had changed.

The box of mix was tucked behind an unopened bag of lentils she kept meaning to use. She stirred the batter slowly, watching the flour disappear into the milk and eggs. Maple watched her every move like it was a gourmet cooking show made just for her.

When the first pancake hit the pan, Maple sat up straighter.

"Don't get any ideas," Tessa warned, flipping it gently. "These are mine."

But when the stack was done, two golden, slightly lopsided pancakes resting on her favorite blue plate, she looked down and saw Maple's expectant gaze.

Just one bite.

She tore off a small piece, made sure it was cool, and held it out.

Maple sniffed it. Nibbled. Then looked up with eyes that said, More?

Tessa smiled.

"Fine. One small pancake."

She made a third. Silver-dollar sized. Plain. No syrup. Just enough to make it a moment.

They ate in near silence. Tessa at the table, Maple on the rug beside her, the sound of drizzle tapping against the window like a soft metronome.

Afterward, Maple licked her paws and let out a long, happy sigh.

Tessa refilled her coffee and whispered to the empty kitchen, "I guess we're doing this again next week."

The next Sunday, Maple was already in the kitchen before Tessa was fully awake.

She was sitting in front of the pantry again, waiting.

Tessa didn't question it.

She just reached for the mix.

By the third week, it had a name: *The Sunday Pancake Pact.*

Two for Tessa. One for Maple.

Every week, no matter what.

By mid-November, Maple knew the signs.

Tessa would shuffle into the kitchen wearing her fuzzy gray slippers, hair in a loose braid, and hum something half-forgotten from the radio. That's when Maple sprang into action, trotting over to the pantry like an executive chef checking inventory, tail swaying like it had its own melody.

Sometimes, Tessa would pretend to forget.

She'd pour her coffee, flip through the mail, and ask, "Now, what was I going to do?"

Maple would sit. And wait.

Always by the pantry. Always with the same expression: You know what to do.

And Tessa, smiling despite herself, would say, "Right. Of course."

One Sunday, she made them blueberry pancakes.

She debated whether Maple should have a taste, just one berry mashed, but figured it couldn't hurt. She handed it over with a wink.

"You're spoiled," she said.

Maple responded by licking a bit of batter off Tessa's finger, then curling under the table with her prize.

The house was still quiet. Too quiet, sometimes. Tessa hadn't quite gotten used to it.

The divorce had been final for almost a year, but echoes still lingered. Spaces on the walls where framed photos once hung, drawers with too many empty dividers, echoes in rooms that used to be full of someone else's laughter.

But Sunday mornings felt different now.

Not loud. Not lonely.

Just... full. Of small sounds, soft tail thumps, and the occasional flap of a pancake as it landed on the plate just right.

One particularly chilly morning, Tessa found herself reaching for the good plates. The ones she usually saved for guests. She placed one pancake on each, then sat across from Maple, who was already wagging in slow motion.

"Look at us," she said. "Full service."

Maple licked her lips and let out a single, breathy woof.

It was ridiculous, probably. But it grounded her. This silly, sweet ritual she shared with her dog.

And somehow, it felt like enough.

That afternoon, Tessa bundled up and took Maple for a long walk through the neighborhood. The trees were bare now, leaves gathered in golden piles that Maple trotted through like she was stirring the air.

They passed an older woman raking her yard in thick gloves. She looked up and smiled.

"That's a happy pup you've got there," she called out.

"She had pancakes this morning," Tessa replied before she could stop herself.

The woman laughed. "Did she now?"

Tessa grinned. "It's our thing."

They waved and kept walking, Maple lifting her head a little higher, as if she knew she'd just been bragged about.

Over the next few months, the ritual expanded.

Maple got her own small dish with her name etched on it. Tessa found it online one night after a glass of wine and decided it was worth it. She started lighting a candle on the table too, not for any reason. Just because it made the kitchen feel like a place where nice things happened.

She even tried new pancake variations. Cinnamon. Banana. One week she made oat flour pancakes and spent the whole meal apologizing to Maple, who still ate hers happily.

Tessa started sleeping better.

She looked forward to Sundays.

Not just because of the food. But because of the stillness. The togetherness. The way Maple made everything feel a little less empty, a little more alive.

What surprised her most wasn't how much she needed the ritual.

It was how much Maple seemed to need it, too.

The week drifted by in its usual rhythm: work, errands, quiet dinners for one with the sound of paws nearby.

But by Saturday night, the air felt different.

It was subtle at first, a heaviness in the breeze, a tension in the sky.

By morning, the storm had settled in.

The kind that made everything slow down.

The kind that tiptoed in overnight, bringing heavy skies, wet branches, and an eerie quiet to the street outside.

When Tessa woke, the light filtering through the curtains was soft and bluish, the kind that hinted something wasn't quite right.

She reached for her phone on the nightstand.

Blank screen.

Then she flipped the light switch.

Nothing.

The power was out.

Maple met her at the foot of the bed, tail swishing tentatively. Not her usual bouncy self. She seemed to sense the difference, the odd weight in the air.

Tessa rubbed her forehead and sighed. "Well. I guess today's going to be a little different."

She shuffled to the kitchen, still wearing her robe, and set the coffee mug down with a soft thunk. Out of habit, she reached for the machine before catching herself.

"Right."

She turned to Maple. "No coffee."

Maple blinked.

Tessa pulled back the curtain and looked out into the misty gray morning. A few neighbors were outside, scanning the quiet street. No hum from the usual appliances. No flicker of porch lights.

But it was Sunday.

And Sunday meant pancakes.

Tessa turned to see Maple standing at the edge of the kitchen, head tilted in full anticipation. She was facing the pantry.

Just like always.

Tessa opened her mouth to speak, then closed it again. Instead, she walked over slowly, crouched down, and gently rested her hand on Maple's head.

"I know, sweetheart. I didn't forget."

But without the stove, there could be no pancakes.

No batter sizzling in the pan.

No flipping, no syrup, no candlelight.

Tessa looked around the kitchen, suddenly aware of how much sound their little tradition created. And how strange everything felt now without it.

She stood up, hesitated, then opened the pantry anyway. Maple perked up.

Tessa pulled out the box of mix and set it on the counter. Maple wagged.

"I'm not sure why I'm doing this," she said, smiling despite herself. "We're not exactly cooking today."

But she left it there—just the sight of it made things feel a little more right.

She poured a bowl of kibble for Maple and sliced up half a banana for herself. Then she sat at the table, and Maple curled up nearby.

Not under the table.

Not at her feet.

But right in front of the pantry, as if keeping the faith alive.

They ate in silence.

No pancakes. No sizzle. But still together.

Still Sunday.

After breakfast, Tessa poured herself a thermos of water and lit a match to warm a beeswax candle, one of the emergency ones she kept in the drawer. Its glow was smaller than usual, but it flickered kindly.

She opened her journal to a blank page and wrote:

No pancakes today. But we showed up. Both of us. That has to count for something.

By the afternoon, the power returned with a quiet click and a mechanical hum.

The fridge kicked on.

The coffee machine blinked back to life.

The digital clock on the microwave flashed 12:00.

Tessa didn't rush to make pancakes then. It felt too late, like the window had passed. But Maple stayed near, tail soft and slow, watching her move around the house.

That evening, while folding laundry in front of the TV, Tessa glanced down and saw Maple's nose resting on the edge of the mat.

Waiting.

Quietly.

She smiled.

"You want a raincheck?"

Maple blinked once.

Tessa folded the last towel and stood up.

"Alright, then. Let's have pancakes tomorrow. We'll just call it Monday Brunch."

And they did.

It wasn't the same, exactly. The light felt different. The morning had come and gone. But Maple's tail wagged as she got her pancake, and Tessa felt the same warmth spread across her chest as she sat down at the table.

It didn't have to be perfect.

It just had to be shared.

By the time spring settled in for good, Sunday mornings had become sacred.

It wasn't something Tessa ever wrote down or circled on the calendar. But she felt it in her bones, the way you feel muscle memory before you stretch. The moment she stirred in bed, before her feet hit the floor, Maple was there, waiting by the bedroom door like a soft little reminder: it's time.

And she was right.

Tessa had stopped experimenting with pancake recipes. She'd found her favorite: buttermilk with a hint of cinnamon, just enough to feel special. Maple's got her own plain version, still silver-dollar sized, still warm from the pan, placed with care into the little dish with her name on it.

By now, it wasn't just the food that mattered.

It was the calm. And the company.

The way Maple watched every move. The soft clatter of the mixing spoon. The candle lit by the window. The two of them in a kitchen that had finally started to feel like home.

One Sunday, Tessa heard a knock at the door just as she was flipping the second pancake.

She frowned. Unexpected visitors were rare before 9 a.m., and Maple didn't bark. She just trotted over and sat beside the door with polite curiosity.

It was Tracey from next door, holding a bundle wrapped in a checkered cloth.

"Thought you could use some fresh strawberries," she said. "Picked them up at the farmer's market yesterday."

Tessa smiled. "You're interrupting a sacred ceremony, you know."

"Oh, I know," Tracey grinned. "Maple's weekly pancake blessing."

Tessa laughed. "You joke, but honestly? It's not that far off."

She invited Tracey in for a minute, and Maple sat upright like a little hostess, tail wagging.

"Well," Tracey said, setting the berries on the counter, "guess I should let the ritual continue."

But just before she stepped out, she turned back and said, "You should write about this, you know. The pancakes. The dog. It's a love story."

Tessa raised an eyebrow. "A short one."

"Still counts."

When the door closed, Tessa stood for a moment, hands resting on the counter.

She looked down at Maple, who was already back in her spot by the pantry, ready for pancake number three.

"Maybe she's right," Tessa said, dropping the berries into a colander. "Maybe this is our love story."

Maple licked her lips in agreement.

She added strawberries to her own plate that morning—sliced thin, placed neatly on the side. Maple's stayed the same. Plain, warm, familiar.

Just the way she liked it.

One Sunday in early summer, Maple did something new.

After eating her pancake, instead of curling up on the rug like usual, she trotted over to the hallway, paused, and turned back to look at Tessa.

Her tail gave a small wag.

Tessa wiped her hands on a towel. "What's this? A post-pancake field trip?"

Maple tilted her head.

Tessa followed.

Maple padded into the living room, over to the low windowsill that overlooked the garden. The marigolds were opening now, and the first tomato plant had started to lean a little in the wind.

Tessa opened the window, and Maple hopped up onto the bench beneath it, resting her chin on the ledge.

They stood like that for a while, one sitting, one standing, both of them looking out at the quiet morning.

"Maybe this is part of the pact now," Tessa said softly. "Step one: pancakes. Step two: window watch."

Maple wagged.

And from then on, that's what they did.

Pancakes first.

Then the window bench.

Some mornings, Tessa brought her coffee. Other times, she brought the journal she rarely wrote in anymore, just holding it open in her lap. Maple kept lookout. Occasionally, she let out one soft bark if a squirrel dared to pass through the garden.

It wasn't about guarding the yard.

It was about being there.

Together.

Tessa couldn't quite explain why the ritual mattered so much. She just knew that when she missed it, on the rare Sunday when she had to be away, it felt like something was off-kilter.

It wasn't guilt. Just longing.

Like missing a friend's voice.

Like forgetting your favorite song and remembering it suddenly at a stoplight.

By the time the second summer of the ritual rolled around, Tessa couldn't imagine life without it.

Sunday meant more than pancakes.

It meant intention.

A reason to be soft. A reason to slow down.

She didn't need big plans. Or travel itineraries. Or life milestones to feel fulfilled.

She had Maple.

And the soft, cherished sound of batter hitting a warm pan.

Chapter 6

The Only Warm Thing in the Room

The bed felt too big. Again.

She lay flat on her back, eyes open, watching the slow crawl of headlights across the ceiling. They came and went in silent waves, brushing the walls like ghostly reminders that the world outside still moved. Inside the house, though, time had slowed to a trickle. Or maybe it had stopped entirely. It was hard to tell these days.

The house had been quiet before, like when the kids were at school or at their friend's birthday parties, but this quiet was different. This was *empty* quiet. No leftover laughter. No backpacks dumped by the door. No clutter. No arguments over screen time or which cereal to buy. Just clean counters, soft shadows, and a calendar that reminded her, in its neat little squares, when the weekends weren't hers anymore.

It was Friday night. The kids were with their dad.

And she hated this part.

She shifted under the covers and exhaled into the darkness. Across the room, the heater clicked on, but the warmth didn't reach her. Her chest felt tight and heavy, like grief was a weighted blanket she couldn't kick off.

She didn't cry. She had done enough of that in recent weeks. Enough curled-up-in-the-shower sobs and late-night drives with the radio off. Now the sadness had settled into something quieter. Not better. Just... quieter.

Something shifted beside her.

A soft sigh. The rustle of fur. And then, with practiced ease, a tiny weight scooted closer to her ribcage and flopped with dramatic flair. A warm, peanut-shaped loaf of loyalty.

"Hi, buddy," she whispered.

Peanut didn't respond, of course. He just nestled closer, like his job tonight was to press all ten pounds of himself against the sadness and see if that helped.

And somehow, it did.

She rested a hand on his little back, feeling the steady rise and fall of his breathing. His fur was short and warm, slightly wiry near the spine but soft on his belly. He let out a small grunt when she scratched the spot just behind his left ear. His tail gave a half-hearted wag, the kind that said *I'm listening, but I'm very comfortable, so please don't move again.*

She smiled.

It hadn't been her idea to get a dog. Especially not a small one. She'd always thought of herself as a "big dog" person. Labs, shepherds, golden retrievers. Dogs you could hike with, or throw a stick for at the lake. Dogs that could wear a bandana and look like a movie star.

But when the divorce talks started, and the heaviness began creeping into their home, the kids had begged for something to love. Something happy and simple and new. Something to hold onto. At first, she said no. Then she said maybe. Then, one rainy Saturday in February, she found herself standing in the middle of a crowded animal shelter, clutching a clipboard while her children sat on the floor giggling as a lopsided, bug-eyed creature climbed all over them.

"His name's Peanut," the volunteer had said. "He's part terrier, part... well, something. We're not really sure."

She had crouched down for a better look. Peanut had barked once, sneezed twice, and then proudly dragged a chew toy the size of his entire body across the floor like he owned the place.

"He's so small," she'd murmured.

"Exactly," her daughter had said. "He can sleep in our beds."

Peanut had trotted over, tail wagging furiously, and plopped into her lap like he'd been waiting for her his whole life.

It was over in that moment.

She brought him home that afternoon, still smelling faintly of oatmeal shampoo and shelter air. He'd peed on the welcome mat and howled at the vacuum cleaner, but none of them cared. He belonged.

Now, months later, with the house split and the marriage gone and the kids spending weekends elsewhere, Peanut was still here.

And tonight, he was the only warm thing in the room.

Her fingers moved slowly along his back. He stretched out further, his little legs extending like toothpicks, and yawned without opening his eyes.

"You're such a weirdo," she said softly. "Do you know that?"

Peanut snorted.

She let her head fall back onto the pillow. It smelled faintly of lavender and dryer sheets, things she'd clung to lately, little rituals of comfort. A different brand of tea. A new set of bedsheets. Clean drawers, lit candles, short walks around the block. All the things people said helped. And they did, in their way. But nothing helped quite like this—this tiny heartbeat against her side, this warm presence that never left.

He didn't ask questions. Didn't care whose weekend it was. Didn't judge how many times she'd microwaved frozen dinners or worn the same hoodie for three days in a row.

He just showed up.

Every night, like clockwork, he'd hop up onto the bed with an exaggerated grunt, circle twice, and drop his little body beside hers with the resigned sigh of someone who had taken on a very important job.

And maybe he had.

Maybe this *was* a job. Holding her together in the spaces between what had been and whatever came next.

She looked over at him now, his chin tucked adorably into the fold of the comforter, ears twitching in sleep. His underbite stuck out slightly, as if he were frowning in his dreams.

She remembered, suddenly, the day she'd cried on the kitchen floor. The paperwork had just gone through. The house had been too quiet. She'd sunk down by the fridge, hugging her knees, feeling like everything she knew had slipped out from under her.

Peanut had trotted in, dropped his disgusting squeaky duck toy on her lap, and then crawled into the crook of her arm with the kind of loyalty she didn't think she'd ever earned.

He hadn't tried to fix anything. He'd just stayed.

That was the magic of him.

She pulled the covers up around them both, tucking her arm gently around his warm little body. His ears flicked once, then stilled.

"I didn't want a small dog," she whispered. "But you're not small. Not really."

He didn't stir. Didn't need to.

Because they both knew what she meant.

He was small in size, sure. But somehow, he filled every quiet part of this room. Every aching corner. Every stretch of space that used to hold someone else. He didn't take away the sadness, but he softened it. Made it feel less like an ending, and more like something survivable.

Her chest ached with something tender. Not grief, exactly. Not anymore. More like... gratitude. Quiet and deep.

She adjusted the pillow beneath her head and let her eyes drift closed.

Tomorrow would come with its own noise. Maybe she'd go to the grocery store. Maybe she'd rearrange the bookshelf. Maybe she'd miss the kids so much her ribs would feel hollow. But for now, for this hour, this bed, and this dog, she had what she needed.

Peanut shifted once more, then settled completely, his little snore rising into the room like a lullaby.

And she breathed, for the first time that day, without effort.

The bed was still big. The house was still quiet. The ache was still there.

But so was he.

The only warm thing in the room.

And somehow, that was enough.

Chapter 7

She Snores Louder Than Me

I t started with one night.

One chilly, restless night when I thought, *She looks so cold down there on the floor,* and I patted the edge of the bed like some overly generous queen bestowing a royal invitation.

"Just for tonight," I said aloud.

She didn't hesitate. Not even a second of canine modesty. She leapt up like she'd been waiting her whole life for that moment.

And just like that, the bed was no longer mine.

The first thing you need to know is this: she's not a small dog.

She's not one of those delicate fluffballs who curls into the corner like a croissant.

No. She's a sprawler. A lanky, leggy, 60-pound mutt with no respect for pillow zones, personal space, or the laws of gravity. She doesn't lie *on* the bed so much as she becomes the bed.

And she snores.

Not dainty snuffles. No soft little puffs.

We're talking full-throttle, construction-site-level snoring. With grunts. With occasional growls. And once, just once, but I swear I'm not making this up, a honk that sounded exactly like a goose with sinus issues.

But we'll get to that.

Let's start at the beginning.

Before her, I had rules.

Firm, no-nonsense rules.

No dogs on the bed. No dogs on the couch. No dogs in the bathroom while I was brushing my teeth because it made me feel like I was performing for an audience.

I liked my space.

I liked clean sheets and quiet nights and knowing that I could roll over at 2 a.m. without ending up nose-to-nose with a snoring fur monster.

And then came Hazel.

Adopted on a whim after a rough breakup and an even rougher winter. She was shy at first, polite. The kind of dog who asked permission with her eyes before stepping into a room. I admired her boundaries. She respected mine.

For about a week.

Then came The Bed Incident.

That night, it was colder than usual. The wind made that eerie sound through the old vent in my room, the kind of sound that makes you wrap the blanket tighter even if you're already warm.

Hazel was curled on the floor on her thrift-store dog bed, looking like the picture of canine sadness. Just a big, sleepy question mark of fur.

And I... well, I caved.

"One night," I said, patting the bed. "That's it."

She didn't need convincing. She bounded up, circled three times, and flopped down across my shins with the grace of a falling oak tree.

It was like sleeping under a warm, heavy bag of rice.

But that was the night I slept better than I had in months.

Of course, one night turned into two.

Then a week.

Then, suddenly, it felt wrong when she wasn't there.

There's something oddly comforting about having a dog in bed.

The rhythmic breathing. The soft weight against your back. The way they somehow know when your dreams get too loud and nuzzle closer like they're anchoring you to the present.

Even the snoring, once you get used to it, becomes background music. A weird, wheezy lullaby.

But here's the thing no one warns you about: dogs take over.

Not dramatically. Not all at once.

They do it gradually. Strategically.

First, they wedge themselves between your knees.

Then they scoot higher, until you find yourself clinging to the edge of the mattress like a shipwreck survivor while they stretch out like a lazy emperor across the middle.

And forget about blankets.

Hazel is a professional cover thief. She's got this technique: one powerful back leg kick and *whoosh*, the blanket's gone, pulled into a tangle around her like she's recreating a renaissance painting.

I wake up freezing, blanketless, clinging to the corner with half my pillow hanging off the bed while she's swaddled like a burrito and snoring like a chainsaw.

I've tried to reclaim space.

I've pushed gently. Shifted her. Tried the "stern whisper" method at 2 a.m. You know, the voice where you're trying not to wake the whole neighborhood but still want to sound authoritative.

"Hazel. Move."

She'll lift her head slightly, blink once, and then flop right back down. On my hip. Or my foot. Or, once memorably, on my actual face.

But the thing is... it's funny. Endearing, even.

It's hard to stay mad when she snores mid-dream and kicks the air like she's chasing something glorious in her sleep.

Or when she stretches in the morning, tail tapping gently, before flopping her head onto my chest like I'm her favorite pillow.

She has no concept of "personal space," but she has perfected "personal presence."

And her presence has filled my nights with something I didn't know I was missing.

There are other perks, too.

Hazel is the perfect foot warmer.

She never cares if I go to bed in mismatched socks or with a face mask that makes me look like a mint-colored swamp creature.

She's a surprisingly good listener when I ramble before bed, muttering about to-do lists or that thing I forgot to say in a meeting.

She doesn't offer advice.

She just sighs, deeply, like she gets it.

And somehow, it settles something in me.

Of course, there are the nights when she dreams too hard and kicks me in the ribs.

Or the times she flops onto her back, paws in the air, and takes up 75 percent of the mattress while I lie curled at the edge, trying not to fall off.

And let's not forget the snoring.

It really is... impressive.

I've downloaded sleep apps to track the decibels.

Once, the app thought I lived next to a highway.

I don't.

I live with Hazel.

Who, despite being a medium-sized mutt with a gentle soul, snores like a diesel engine.

And somehow... that's just become part of my life.

One night, I had the flu.

Full-on chills, fever, the works.

I came home, collapsed into bed, and pulled the covers over my head, hoping the world would go away.

Hazel climbed up gently.

Not her usual full-body flop, but slow, careful, deliberate.

She curled beside me, pressing her back against mine.

No snoring that night.

Just quiet breath. Warmth.

Every time I shifted, she did too.

And I remember thinking, in the fog of fever and exhaustion, *This dog takes up all my space... but also holds all my heart.*

She's snoring now, actually.

Flat on her side, one paw twitching, her tail giving a slow wag every so often.

The blankets are halfway off me, but I don't mind.

I've learned to sleep in weird positions. Learned to share the pillow. Learned to cherish the weight of her pressed against my legs like a reminder that I'm never truly alone.

It's not the sleep I imagined.

It's better.

Messier. Warmer. Furrier.

But better.

Some nights, I lie there and think about what life was like before her.

Before the bed became a shared kingdom of tangled blankets and sideways paws. Before I had to vacuum the comforter weekly or wake up with dog breath fogging my nose.

It was neater then. Quieter. Less chaotic.

But it was also… lonelier.

There's something about a dog that fills in the spaces you didn't know were empty.

Hazel doesn't fix the hard things. She doesn't stop the work stress, the family drama, the weird ache that sometimes sits right in the center of my chest for no reason at all.

But she's there.

Always there.

And some nights, when the world feels heavy, her snoring is oddly comforting.

It's like the universe is saying, "See? Some things are still simple. Still soft."

Of course, not everyone gets it.

My sister visited last fall and spent a night on the pull-out couch.

In the morning, I found her in the kitchen, eyes bleary, sipping coffee like it was medicine.

"She snores louder than you," she said flatly.

I blinked. "Who?"

"Your dog. Hazel. I thought there was construction happening in the vents."

I tried not to laugh. "You get used to it."

She gave me a long look. "Do you?"

I shrugged. "Eventually."

Later that week, I caught her sneaking Hazel a piece of toast under the table.

Even the skeptics fall for her.

We've developed a bedtime routine now.

Hazel waits patiently while I brush my teeth, then trots to the bed ahead of me, hops up, and turns exactly three tight circles before flopping down.

She always starts on my side of the bed.

Always.

I'll lift the blanket and say, "Excuse me, ma'am, that's *my* spot."

She'll stare at me for a moment, the whites of her eyes showing just enough to be funny, then sigh and scoot approximately three millimeters.

Sometimes I give up and contort myself around her.

Sometimes I play the long game, turning off the lights and waiting until she moves of her own accord.

It's a delicate dance.

A nightly negotiation.

And honestly? I wouldn't trade it for anything.

One night last winter, the power went out.

No lights. No heat. Just darkness and silence, broken only by the wind knocking at the windows.

I lit candles. Found the old quilt in the closet. Crawled into bed with Hazel already snuggled in like a living hot water bottle.

As I settled under the covers, she shifted closer, rested her head on my leg, and let out one of those long, soul-deep sighs she saves for moments of total contentment.

There we were. No screens, no sound, just the two of us in the quiet glow of candlelight.

I listened to her breathe.

And for the first time in a long while, I felt completely, perfectly safe.

Hazel's getting older now.

It sneaks up, doesn't it?

The graying muzzle, the slower mornings, the way she pauses at the bottom of the bed before climbing up like it takes more effort than it used to.

Sometimes she misses the jump entirely and gives me this look like, *A little help, please?*

And I do. Every time.

Because she's carried me, too.

Through heartbreaks. Through holidays spent alone. Through long stretches of ordinary days that would've blurred together without her warm, goofy, chaotic presence.

So now, when she needs a boost, I give it.

When her snoring is louder than ever and rattles the walls?

I smile into the darkness and think, *That's my girl.*

She's more than a bedmate now.

She's a bedtime ritual.

A source of laughter when I find her belly-up with all four paws twitching like she's in the middle of an epic squirrel chase.

A silent listener when I whisper half-thoughts into the night.

A breathing reminder that life doesn't have to be perfect to be beautiful.

A few weeks ago, I had one of those nights where I just couldn't sleep.

My mind was racing: work stress, family things, the usual spiral of "what ifs" that show up when the lights go out.

I tossed. Turned. Huffed into my pillow.

Hazel stayed quiet for a long time.

But around 2 a.m., she shuffled closer. Pressed her head against my chest. One paw draped across my stomach.

She didn't snore that night.

Didn't even breathe heavily.

She just... stayed.

Still. Steady. Present.

And eventually, so did I.

Some people think dogs are messy.

And they're not wrong.

Hazel has taken over my bed, my couch, my laundry basket, and my heart.

She drools when she sleeps.

She sheds year-round.

She farts in her sleep and then acts offended like *I* did it.

But she's also shown me how beautiful it is to share your space with someone who gives their whole heart without hesitation.

Who doesn't care about boundaries because they've decided you're family.

Who steals the covers, hogs the pillows, and still manages to give you the best sleep of your life.

And yes. She snores louder than me.

Much louder.

But after all this time, I've come to find that I can't sleep quite right without it.

Her snoring is the sound of home now.

It's her saying, *I'm here. You're safe. Let's rest.*

And I do.

We do.

Every single night.

Chapter 8

The Waiting Is the Hardest Part

Maya had walked to the window for the fifth time in ten minutes.

There was nothing new to see, just the same slow movement of clouds and the quiet street below, but it gave her somewhere to stand, something to do. The apartment, usually a comfort, now felt too still. Too quiet. Too wrong.

Gracie wasn't here.

Gracie was in surgery.

She moved from the window to the couch, sat for ten seconds, then stood again. Her pacing had worn a loop through the living room that she couldn't seem to break. Every time she sat, her hands started to shake. So she moved. Back to the kitchen. Back to the window. Back to the memory of Gracie limping across the yard with her tail still wagging.

That was what made it worse. The wag.

Even with a torn ACL, even in pain, Gracie had looked at her with that expectant sparkle, her beloved colorful ball between her teeth, practically begging, *Just one more throw? Please? Just one more?*

Maya hadn't known it was serious at first. Gracie was always a little clumsy, more fluff than coordination. But after that chase, she wouldn't put weight on her back leg. Not when she came inside. Not after dinner. Not the next morning either.

The vet had said surgery was necessary. ACL tears were common, especially in small dogs like Gracie. It was a clean tear. Fixable. But it would be a long recovery.

And so here they were.

Gracie was at the animal hospital.

And Maya was pacing a hole in the floor.

Her phone sat on the coffee table like it might ring if she stared at it long enough. She checked the time. 10:47. She'd dropped Gracie off at 9.

This wasn't the first time she had felt helpless in a hospital waiting room, or in this case, her own living room pretending to be one. It was the same hollow feeling she remembered from her mom's final days, the kind that sat under your ribs and made breathing feel like work.

She closed her eyes and leaned her forehead against the cool glass of the window.

Gracie.

God, she loved that dog.

She hadn't known she could love something this much, not until the moment she first held her.

Maya had always wanted a dog.

Not in a fleeting, wouldn't-it-be-cute kind of way, but deeply. For as long as she could remember. The kind of wanting that settled in young and never really let go.

But her mom hated dogs.

Too messy. Too loud. Too much work.

So Maya grew up in a house that was tidy, quiet, and decidedly pet-free.

Then came college. Then grad school. Then the research fellowship in Pittsburgh.

She was only supposed to be there for two years, and the plan was always to move back home to her boyfriend, her family, and the familiarity she missed.

But there were rules in that life. No dogs, for one. Her boyfriend didn't want the hair, the hassle, the responsibility. And for a while, she told herself that was fine. That love meant compromise. That this dream could wait.

But as the second year of the fellowship crept in, so did the truth: there were no jobs for her back home. And he didn't want to move.

They broke up quietly. No drama, no yelling. Just a shared understanding that the future they'd imagined didn't fit anymore.

And for the first time in years, Maya asked herself what she really wanted.

The answer came faster than she expected.

A dog.

She started researching that night. Breed info, temperament charts, training guides. She knew exactly what she was looking for: small, fluffy, affectionate. A dog that would be happy in an apartment. One that would follow her from room to room like a shadow with a heartbeat.

Within a week, she found a breeder two hours away with a new litter of Maltese puppies that would be ready for homes in just a few weeks.

Maya sent an inquiry.

The photos came the next day.

There, nestled in a row of fuzzy siblings, was a tiny white pup with big dark eyes and an expression that looked equal parts curious and unbothered.

She drove up that weekend.

The breeder placed the puppy in her arms, and Maya didn't speak for a full minute. The dog looked up at her, blinked once, then curled into her elbow like she'd done it a hundred times before.

She named her Gracie. Not for grace, ironically, because the dog had none, but because her mom had once told her that when life feels too heavy, "you have to look for grace wherever you can."

And in that moment, that's what the dog felt like. A tiny, wiggly kind of grace.

She'd thrown a little puppy party that first night, just her and a few friends from work. They brought squeaky toys and takeout and one of them had a boxer mix puppy that spent the whole night licking Gracie's face. Gracie had zoomed around the living room with the joy of something discovering the world one rug at a time.

From that night on, they were inseparable.

Gracie had gone with her everywhere, from coffee runs to library marathons to one ill-advised attempt to sneak her into a lecture hall inside a tote bag. Through it all, Gracie had been the one steady thing, always ready to snuggle, to listen, and to nudge her hand when the tears came.

And now Gracie was under anesthesia.

And Maya couldn't do a thing about it.

She sat back down on the couch, this time curling her legs beneath her. She reached for Gracie's favorite ball, the one that had started all of this. It was soft, chewed, and smelled faintly of peanut butter. Gracie only chased this one. Other balls were completely ignored. But this one? This one she would bring to bed if allowed. She would carry it from room to room like it was treasure.

The memory made her smile.

She could still see it, Gracie darting into the yard, ears bouncing, snatching the ball mid-bounce with a proud huff. That last time, she'd landed funny. Limped back. But even as she'd stood with her leg up, she'd looked at Maya like, *Come on, I can still go. I've got one more in me.*

That was Gracie. Always more love than body. Always trying.

The phone rang.

She jumped.

The screen lit up: *Vet Clinic.*

Her breath caught in her throat as she answered.

"Hi. This is Dr. Feldman. Just wanted to let you know Gracie is out of surgery and she did great. Everything went smoothly, and she's starting to wake up now. You'll be able to pick her up this afternoon."

She choked out a thank you, tried to sound calm, professional, like she hadn't been counting the seconds. But when she hung up, the tears came fast and hot.

Gracie was okay.

She pressed the ball to her chest and let the relief shake through her.

The vet tech brought Gracie out carefully, cradling her like a baby. Her leg was shaved, covered in neat little stitches and a soft blue bandage. She looked woozy, dazed, her usual bounce dulled by medication. But when she saw Maya, her tail gave a faint, sleepy wag.

Maya felt her heart split wide open.

"Oh, Gracie girl," she whispered, taking her into her arms.

Gracie smelled like antiseptic and cotton. Her fur was patchy from the shave. But she nuzzled into her shoulder and gave the softest sigh of recognition.

"You're coming home," she said. "I've got you."

The recovery wasn't easy.

Maya set up a little bed for Gracie in the living room, surrounded by blankets, her favorite toys, and an absurdly priced orthopedic cushion from an online rabbit hole of "post-op care essentials." She set alarms for medications, wrapped pills in peanut butter, and tracked every stretch, every tiny limp, every tail wag.

There were setbacks, nights where Gracie whimpered in her sleep, days where she wouldn't eat. But there were small victories too. A tail wag. A nose nuzzle. A slow, determined crawl toward the ball she wasn't allowed to chase just yet.

Through it all, the memories came.

Of driving home with her asleep on the passenger seat the first day they met. Of late nights writing papers with Gracie curled against her hip. Of that time during the pandemic when she'd danced around the kitchen to stay sane, and Gracie had barked like she was cheering her on.

Maya had never loved anything the way she loved this dog.

And now, every act of care felt like a way to say thank you. For all the years Gracie had quietly held her together. For every morning she woke up to a wet nose and a heartbeat beside her. For the ways she'd taught her to stay when it was hard, to rest when she needed to, and to love without conditions.

Weeks passed.

The fur began to grow back. The limp lessened. Gracie started venturing a little further with each walk, cautiously testing her limits, tail up like a little white flag of hope.

One afternoon, as they sat in the yard together, Gracie nudged the faded colorful ball toward her with her nose.

Maya laughed.

"Not yet," she said gently, picking it up and kissing her head. "But soon."

Gracie gave her a look that said, *I'll be ready.*

And Maya believed her.

She lay back in the grass, Gracie curled beside her, and let the sun warm her face.

This dog had carried her through so many chapters. And now, it was her turn. To carry Gracie through this one. To be the steady presence. The constant. The home.

The waiting had been the hardest part.

But love was the easy part.

Always.

Chapter 9

Fifteen Minutes and a Memory

She wasn't supposed to be scrolling.

The plan was to review the deck one more time before the 4:30 Zoom call. But her eyes were tired, her brain was fried, and her fingers had wandered to the Instagram icon on autopilot. Just a quick scroll, she told herself. A two-minute mental break.

And then there it was.

A photo she hadn't seen in years—tagged, not posted. Fuzzy, slightly overexposed, but unmistakable: a chubby yellow puppy with a red bow around his neck, giant paws sprawled across a pile of torn wrapping paper. His tongue was out, mid-pant, eyes bright with chaos and joy.

Her breath caught in her throat.

"Benny," she whispered.

She turned her phone sideways to get a better look. The photo was from her best friend's page, posted the Christmas she got him. It had been reshared today in one of those "On This Day" memory montages that social media liked to surprise people with. She hadn't been expecting it. Certainly not here, in the middle of a workday, half an hour before presenting budget numbers to people in suits.

She swallowed hard and tapped the photo, holding it closer to her face like it might offer something more. Her heart thumped against her ribs.

God, he was *so* small.

She glanced at the clock. 4:15.

Fifteen minutes left.

She could still pull it together. She just needed a breath, a sip of water, maybe a sticky note of bullet points to fake preparedness. But instead, she swiped again. And again. And then she was in it, fully in it, the rabbit hole of puppy pictures she didn't know she needed.

There he was in the laundry basket, surrounded by warm towels. There he was gnawing on the corner of the coffee table. In one picture, he was fast asleep in a pile of her scarves, a tiny furry ball with a snoring problem.

She smiled and exhaled through her nose, not quite a laugh.

She could still remember the way he smelled back then. Not just the puppy breath, but the mix of cedar chips and oatmeal shampoo and something sweet and warm and alive.

The Christmas she got Benny was not a good Christmas.

It had been three weeks since her dad died. Everything felt dim. The lights on the tree were too bright. The cinnamon candle made her nauseous. Even the wrapping paper felt too loud. Her boyfriend at the time, Matt, had tried his best. He made her dinner, poured her wine, tried to keep the TV playing lighthearted stuff. But grief had wrapped around her like a wet blanket. Heavy. Cold. Clingy.

And then he came out of the bedroom holding a squirming yellow blur with a ribbon tied around his neck.

"I know it won't fix anything," Matt had said. "But... I thought maybe it would help."

She hadn't spoken. Just held him. This awkward, floppy, whimpering little pup with fur like vanilla pudding and eyes too big for his head.

"He's yours," Matt had said softly. "I named him Benny."

Her throat had closed up at that. Benny was her dad's nickname, short for Bernard. She'd grown up hearing it yelled across baseball fields and whispered on long car rides and scribbled on post-its with terrible dad handwriting.

Naming the dog Benny was the kindest thing Matt ever did.

And maybe the most permanent.

Matt wasn't in her life anymore. The breakup had been surprisingly clean, a mutual understanding that they had tried, and it hadn't lasted. She'd kept the apartment. He kept the camping gear. There was no yelling, no betrayal. Just... the quiet kind of ending that feels more like a door slowly closing.

But Benny had stayed.

For eight years, he had stayed.

The yellow fur had lightened around his snout. The puppy belly was gone. But he was still her boy. Her shadow. Her reason for getting out of bed on weekends when the world felt too loud. The one who greeted her every day like she'd just returned from war.

4:21.

She blinked hard and set her phone down, the screen going dark beside her keyboard. She turned her chair toward the window and stared at the city street below. People were still moving. Still going about their errands, their commutes, their lives. She wondered how many of them were holding onto someone like she held onto Benny. Not out of desperation, but out of quiet gratitude.

He was her constant. Her little bit of calm in a life that had seen more than its fair share of chaos.

She thought of him now, probably asleep on the couch in that ridiculous position he liked, legs in the air, jowls drooping, one paw twitching with dreams of chasing things he never actually chased. He didn't bark much. Didn't chew anymore. Mostly, he just followed her from room to room, flopped wherever she landed, and made the house feel less empty.

He had been there through job changes, breakups, friendships that faded, birthdays she didn't want to celebrate, and mornings that started with tears in the shower. He had watched her pace the kitchen floor on long phone calls and sat beside her on the porch while she talked to her dad's memory like he could still hear her.

Benny had never once asked for anything other than a walk, a scratch behind the ears, and a slice of cheese when she made sandwiches.

She thought about how she had left that morning in a rush—keys in one hand, travel mug in the other, apologizing as she closed the door.

"Back soon," she'd said, kissing his head. "Last meeting's at four."

4:24.

She smiled now, a soft, private thing that didn't touch her eyes.

She wasn't excited about the meeting. She wasn't even prepared for it, truth be told. But she was very, *very* ready for what came after.

The walk home. The jingle of his collar when he heard the key in the door. The way he'd dance in tiny circles, tail sweeping the air like a metronome of joy.

And then, dinner for two. Not fancy. Just her and Benny, eating in the living room like they always did. He'd sit beside her on the rug, waiting patiently for a bite of whatever she was eating, even if it was just scrambled eggs and toast. And then later, they'd curl up on the couch. Maybe she'd talk to him. Maybe she'd read. Maybe she'd say nothing at all.

And he'd stay right there.

Her anchor. Her history. Her heart.

4:28.

She wiped the corner of her eye with her sleeve and clicked open her presentation. The spreadsheet looked suddenly less intimidating. The talking points less important.

She wasn't sad, exactly. Just full. Brimming. A heart caught between memory and presence. Between what was lost and what stayed.

The meeting would end by five. And then she'd go home.

To Benny.

To the one who never left.

Chapter 10

The Baby Blanket Test

Nora stood in the nursery doorway, holding a pale green blanket to her chest.

She hadn't meant to stop here. She was just passing through the hall on her way to fold laundry when she caught the edge of the crib out of the corner of her eye. The room had that quiet, unfinished stillness, half-lived in and half-imagined. Stacks of books waited to be shelved. A baby mobile sat in its box, unopened. The scent of fresh paint lingered faintly, like the memory of a recent decision.

She stepped inside without meaning to.

The blanket was soft, flannel, with tiny embroidered stars stitched into the border. It was the first thing she bought after the test turned positive. Not a necessity. Not even practical. Just something she saw in the store and reached for, almost unconsciously, like her hands had known before her mind did. She hadn't even told Liam yet. That came later.

Nora smoothed the blanket over the edge of the crib and stood back.

Max padded in behind her, quiet as always.

He'd been that way since the beginning, gentle, observant, never pushy. At six years old, Max still moved with the same quiet curiosity he had as a puppy. His golden coat shimmered in the afternoon light, and his tail wagged in a slow arc, not excited, just... aware. A steady rhythm, like a heartbeat you could see.

Nora knelt down and scratched behind his ear.

"You know something's coming, don't you?"

Max responded the way he always did: with eyes that understood more than she could explain.

She hadn't expected to feel so unsure.

Everyone had said Max would be fine. "Goldens are great with babies," her sister had said. "They're practically nannies." Even the vet had smiled when she'd asked. "He'll probably be obsessed with the baby," she'd said. "They get protective. Loving. You'll see."

Still.

There were moments, like this one, where doubt crept in.

He'd been her baby for so long. Her companion. Her rhythm keeper. When Liam traveled for work or her migraines kept her curled under a blanket all day, Max had been there. He didn't ask for anything except to be near her. He understood quiet.

Would he understand a baby's cry?

Would he feel replaced?

Nora sat down on the rug, cross-legged beside him. Max rested his head on her knee with a sigh, the weight of him warm and familiar.

She looked around the room again. The crib. The changing table. The rocking chair she hadn't quite broken in yet.

She reached for the blanket, lifted it gently, and let it settle into Max's lap.

He sniffed it, blinked, then rested his chin on it.

"Well," she whispered, smiling a little, "I guess that's the baby blanket test."

He didn't move. Just closed his eyes and let out another slow exhale, as if to say: This will be fine. I'm right here.

Nora stayed there a while, her hand on his back, feeling the soft rise and fall of his breathing.

Later, after dinner, Liam asked her why she'd moved the blanket.

She was rinsing dishes, watching Max lie sprawled across the kitchen rug in his usual post-meal coma.

"No reason," she said. "Just checking something."

He didn't ask what.

The truth felt too small to explain. It wasn't really about the blanket. It was about what it meant, this new chapter, this shift in their little family. She wasn't worried in any big, dramatic way. Just quietly. Softly. In the way people worry when they're waiting for their lives to change.

Max followed her into the bedroom as she turned out the lights.

It was his routine. He'd curl at the foot of the bed or beside her nightstand, always within arm's reach.

But that night, when she sat on the edge of the bed to put lotion on her hands, he climbed up next to her.

Not in a demanding way. Just... present.

She looked at him.

"Do you need extra reassurance, or do I?" she asked.

Max leaned into her, pressing his side against her thigh.

Nora smiled and set down the lotion.

They fell asleep that way—him curled against her legs, the hum of the ceiling fan overhead, and the soft, steady comfort of knowing that whatever came next, they'd face it together.

Even if neither of them quite knew how yet.

By the time the crib sheets were washed and folded, Max had claimed the nursery rug as his favorite nap spot.

It started as a fluke. Nora had found him there one afternoon, sprawled out on his side, tail flicking slightly as he dreamed. At first, she assumed he was following the sunlight, which slanted across the floor just so in the early hours. But even on cloudy mornings, he returned to that spot, curling up near the base of the rocking chair.

She didn't tell him to move.

She didn't tell him much of anything anymore.

The closer she got to her due date, the more the words seemed to dry up. Friends checked in regularly, offering freezer meal recipes, car seat hacks, and unsolicited advice about sleep training. Liam did his best, reading books with furrowed brows and assembling furniture with quiet determination, but even his steady presence couldn't completely silence the low hum of anticipation Nora carried in her chest.

Max didn't offer advice.

He didn't ask how she was feeling. He didn't glance nervously at the stack of unopened baby books or suggest they go over their hospital checklist again.

He just followed her.

To the bathroom in the middle of the night. To the kitchen when she craved cereal at 3 a.m. To the front porch when she needed air but didn't want to be alone.

If she moved slowly, he matched her pace.

If she sighed, he looked up.

She started reading aloud to him in the evenings, curled on the couch with her feet up and her hand resting on the curve of her belly. She read from baby books, novels, even product instructions she had no intention of following.

"This swaddle says it's foolproof," she told him once. "But I'm fairly certain I'm the exception."

Max blinked, unimpressed.

When the baby kicked, he looked startled the first time. Then curious. Then calm.

He'd lay his head on her lap and lift his eyes toward her belly as if listening for something only he could hear.

"You'll be gentle," she told him one night. "Won't you?"

Max rested his paw on her knee.

That was all she needed.

Still, some part of her braced. People told stories of pets who grew jealous, acted out, withdrew. Nora tried not to let those stories take up too much room in her mind, but they lingered anyway, like shadows that didn't quite disappear with the light.

In the final weeks, Max stuck closer than ever. If she took too long getting up, he'd nose her elbow gently, as if asking, You okay?

She was. Mostly.

Tired, swollen, slightly terrified... but okay.

One evening, about two weeks before her due date, Nora sat on the nursery floor, folding onesies while Max watched from the doorway.

"These are so small," she whispered, holding up a tiny shirt that looked like it could fit a doll. "Too small to belong to a real person."

She set it down and ran her fingers over the folded blanket in the crib. The stars seemed softer somehow, like they'd faded a little just from being held so often.

She looked at Max.

"Do you think I'm ready?"

Max didn't move.

Didn't blink.

But his tail thumped once against the floor.

She took that as a yes.

That night, as she settled into bed, Max curled up by her side, tucking himself close. She reached over and laid her hand on his head, thumb stroking the spot between his ears.

"Soon," she whispered. "Things are going to be different."

He exhaled slowly, already asleep.

Nora's water broke on a Tuesday morning.

It wasn't dramatic. No sudden gush or movie-style chaos. Just a quiet realization as she stepped out of the shower that something was... different.

She called Liam. Called the doctor. Texted her sister to come stay with Max.

"Be good," she said to him as she grabbed her bag, bending awkwardly to kiss his head. "You'll be the first to know everything."

Max stood at the door as they left, tail still, eyes steady.

The birth was long. Not terrible, not traumatic, just long. Hours blurred into shifts of nurses, whispered reassurances, and soft beeping monitors. When the baby finally arrived, pink and blinking and louder than any human had a right to be, Nora felt everything and nothing all at once.

Liam cried. She laughed. Then cried too.

They named her Sophie.

She had Nora's nose and Liam's serious brow. She was small and perfect and somehow completely unfamiliar.

Nora held her in the quiet moments, skin to skin, letting the world narrow to breath and warmth and heartbeat.

But she kept thinking about Max.

Not in a guilty way. Just... wondering.

Would he understand?

Would he still come find her in the morning?

Would he still curl beside her at night?

They stayed in the hospital two days. Nora slept in short bursts. Sophie made small sounds that felt impossibly loud. Liam texted updates to family and friends. Her sister sent pictures of Max lying by the front door, waiting.

"He hasn't budged," the caption read.

Nora stared at the photo until her eyes blurred.

On the third afternoon, they packed up and drove home.

The house smelled like lemons and the faint trace of the vanilla candle Nora always forgot to blow out. The sun filtered through the kitchen window, catching motes of dust in the air. Everything felt smaller. Quieter. Familiar, but changed.

Her sister opened the door with a wide smile, but it was Max Nora looked for.

He came slowly down the hall.

Not bounding. Not barking.

Just walking. Careful. Deliberate.

Nora knelt down, even though her body protested.

Max reached her, pressed his nose gently into her arm, and then paused. Looked past her.

At the bundle in Liam's arms.

His tail twitched once.

"Come say hi," Nora said softly.

Max took one step, then another.

Liam crouched, shifting Sophie's blanket slightly to reveal her tiny face.

Max sniffed.

Long and slow.

Then sat down.

Sophie shifted, made a soft noise, and Max's ears perked.

But he didn't move away.

Nora exhaled, her heart doing something strange and wide in her chest.

She reached for Max's collar, ran her fingers over the tag, and whispered, "Good boy."

He didn't wag.

Not yet.

But he stayed.

That night, after everyone had gone and the dishes were stacked but not washed and Sophie finally slept in her bassinet beside the bed, Nora sat in the rocker with Max lying at her feet.

"You passed," she told him quietly.

He looked up.

"The baby blanket test. You passed it."

Max blinked slowly.

She reached down and touched his paw.

"I'm not worried anymore."

He closed his eyes, the way he always did when he trusted the moment was safe.

The days that followed were a blur of soft cries, swaddled naps, lukewarm coffee, and lists Nora could no longer remember writing.

Sophie slept in small fits, as newborns do, never quite long enough for Nora to believe it would last. She was beautiful, yes, but also loud and needy in ways that caught Nora off guard. There were moments, standing in the kitchen at 2:00 a.m. trying to remember how the bottle warmer worked, when she felt like she was unraveling, thread by thread.

And Max was always there.

Never in the way. Never demanding. Just... near.

If Sophie cried, he looked to Nora first. If Nora cried, sometimes silently, sometimes not, he'd nudge her hand with his nose or lean his body close until she remembered to breathe again.

It wasn't that Nora didn't love her daughter. She did. Fiercely. From the moment Sophie was placed in her arms, she felt something lock into place she hadn't even known was missing.

But loving wasn't the same as knowing what to do.

And sometimes, when the baby wouldn't stop crying or the house felt like it belonged to someone else entirely, Max was the only thing that still made sense.

One afternoon, about three weeks in, Nora sat in the nursery with Sophie asleep on her chest. She hadn't meant to nap—she'd just been rocking, slow and rhythmic, when her eyes had slipped closed.

She woke to the soft sound of Max's tail brushing the floor.

He was lying at her feet, head on his paws, watching them both.

She smiled, groggy and grateful.

"I know, buddy," she whispered.

Max blinked, patient as always.

She reached down and touched the tip of his ear, the familiar curve grounding her in the moment.

They sat like that for a while—mother, child, and dog—all breathing in a kind of fragile rhythm that felt, for once, enough.

Later, Nora found herself reaching for the green blanket.

It had been folded neatly on the shelf for weeks, untouched since before Sophie arrived. But that day, something drew her to it.

She laid it out on the living room floor like a soft little island and placed Sophie in the center, swaddled and blinking at the ceiling fan.

Max watched.

Then, without invitation, he padded over, lay down beside the blanket, and placed his paw—gently, deliberately—just at the corner.

Nora didn't move. Didn't speak.

She just watched the way he curled around Sophie like a question answered.

Max didn't lick. Didn't nuzzle. Just stayed.

It became a ritual.

Every afternoon, after Sophie's second nap, Nora would lay her on the blanket and Max would join her. Sometimes, Nora would lie beside them too. Other times, she'd just sit with her tea and breathe.

Max would stay until Sophie stirred. Then he'd rise, stretch, and walk to the window to look out, as if to say, *My shift is done.*

Nora began to believe, in the quiet spaces between diapers and burp cloths and sleepy bottle feeds, that this might actually work. That love didn't have to divide to stretch.

It could fold outward. It could grow.

Even at 4:00 a.m. when her shirt was stained and her eyelids burned, when Sophie wouldn't latch and Liam mumbled something half-asleep that made no sense at all, even then, when everything felt too much, Max would find her in the hallway, tail softly thumping, and lead her back to bed.

They were figuring it out.

One tiny, imperfect moment at a time.

One morning, about six weeks in, Nora laid Sophie on the blanket and stepped into the kitchen to refill her coffee. She was gone maybe thirty seconds.

When she came back, Max was lying beside the baby with his nose pressed lightly to her sock-covered foot.

Sophie, wide-eyed, stared at him like he was the moon.

"Max..." Nora whispered.

He didn't move. Didn't look at her.

He just stayed there, still as stone, until Sophie hiccupped, then yawned. Then, miraculously, smiled.

Nora's heart cracked open in a way she hadn't expected.

She didn't grab her phone. Didn't take a picture.

She just watched. Watched the two beings she loved most discover each other, in a sunlit room, on a soft green blanket that had once been a question and now felt like an answer.

That night, she told Liam what she saw.

He smiled, rubbing his eyes.

"He's a good dog," he said.

Nora nodded.

"No," she whispered. "He's more than that."

Sophie was eight months old when she finally noticed the tag on Max's collar.

She had just learned to crawl, barely, and moved more like a determined inchworm than a child with motor control. But that morning, with Nora watching from the couch, Sophie reached Max's side, grabbed for the jingling sound she'd heard since birth, and wrapped her chubby fingers around the pewter disc.

Max didn't flinch.

He turned his head slowly, looked at her, and then let her tug—

once, twice—before leaning in, licking her forehead with one gentle swipe of his tongue.

Sophie squealed, delighted.

Nora blinked back tears she didn't fully expect.

It had become so natural, this arrangement. Max was no longer just part of the family, he was part of Sophie's origin story. Her guardian. Her observer. Her first best friend.

When she learned to sit up, it was Max who lay nearby, tail wagging like a drumbeat of encouragement. When she took her first steps, wobbly and wide-eyed, she clutched his fur for balance. He never moved. Not even when she used his tail as a rope. Not even when she tried to feed him soggy cereal from her high chair.

He simply let her.

And Nora, in her quiet way, noticed it all.

Max had always been calm. But this was something else. A kind of reverence.

Like he understood she was his from the beginning.

Sophie's first word was "mama," but her second was "Mah."

She'd call it out from her crib in the mornings, standing in sleep-rumpled pajamas, looking directly at Max where he lay waiting at the door.

And he'd come.

Always.

Some mornings, Nora found them together on the nursery rug before she'd even had her coffee. Sophie babbling nonsense,

Max lying with his head on his paws, listening like every syllable mattered.

The green blanket had been washed so many times it no longer held its shape. The stars had faded, some of the stitching had loosened. But Sophie still reached for it when she was tired, and Max still lay beside it like it was sacred ground.

One rainy afternoon, Nora spread the blanket out again, the way she used to, and Sophie crawled onto it and sat, patting her hand on the soft fabric.

Max circled once, then settled beside her, resting his head in her lap.

Nora watched from the doorway, arms folded over her chest.

She didn't say anything.

Didn't want to break the quiet.

The rain tapped gently against the windows, and in that moment, Nora felt time slow down. Not stop, not pause, but stretch, like the universe was making room for them.

She didn't take a picture.

She didn't call Liam in to see.

She simply stood there and let it imprint.

There would come a time, she knew, when the days would be different. When Sophie would outgrow the blanket. When Max's face would gray a little more. When the magic of now would become the memory of then.

But not today.

Today, they were still here.

All three of them.

Breathing together.

Belonging.

Later that night, after the dishwasher hummed and the house settled into its evening quiet, Nora knelt by Max's bed and placed her hand on his chest.

"You were right, you know," she whispered.

He looked at her, sleepy and content.

"About all of it. From the beginning."

He let out a slow sigh and closed his eyes.

She smiled.

In the nursery, Sophie stirred once, then stilled.

Max didn't move.

He didn't need to anymore.

He knew she was safe.

Years later, when Sophie was four and learning to fold laundry by Nora's side, she pulled the green blanket from the basket.

"This one's mine," she said.

Nora smiled. "It is."

"Max likes it too," Sophie added. "He told me."

Nora didn't question it.

She folded the blanket carefully, pressing her hand over the faded stars, and handed it back to her daughter.

"Why don't you bring it to him?"

Sophie ran off without hesitation, calling his name.

"Mah! Blanket!"

Max, now white-muzzled and slower to stand, wagged his tail and nudged the blanket as Sophie tucked it around him on the rug.

She curled beside him, whispering something only he could hear.

Nora watched from the kitchen, one hand resting on the counter to steady her heart.

So many things had changed.

But Max was still there.

And love, she thought, wasn't measured in milestones or months or how many pictures they managed to take.

Sometimes, love was a faded green blanket.

Sometimes, it was a golden dog who passed every test without even knowing there was one.

And sometimes, it was this:

A child, a dog, and a life that grew in the space between them.

Chapter 11

Window Watchers

She hadn't planned to adopt.

Not at her age. Not at this stage of life, with her knees creaking and mornings slow to start. She wasn't lonely, exactly. She had her books, her tea, her crossword puzzles, and the small rituals that made the days feel full enough. But the house had grown quieter over the years... too quiet, sometimes. Especially in the evenings, when the wind rattled the windows just so and her chair felt too big.

She told herself she was just going to look.

Just to see.

But the moment she stepped into the back row of kennels at the shelter and saw a soft-eyed mutt curled in the corner, white muzzle, thinning coat, a tail that barely moved, something in her shifted.

"She's old," the volunteer said, kneeling beside the gate. "Eleven, maybe twelve. Her name's Mabel."

"Mabel," she repeated, testing the name like a teacup in her hands.

Mabel didn't bark. Didn't stir. Just lifted her head and looked straight into her eyes with the calm of someone who'd seen many things and was in no hurry to be seen herself.

It was not a thunderbolt moment. No swelling music. No instant joy.

Just a quiet understanding.

Two old souls recognizing something familiar.

The first days at home were cautious.

Mabel moved slowly, stiff in her joints, her steps careful and deliberate. She explored one room at a time, nose low to the floor, tail still and watchful.

The woman, whose name was Edith though most people called her Edie, spoke softly, offering Mabel space. A water bowl near the radiator. A thick blanket folded by the bookshelf. Treats placed gently, then walked away from.

It took three days for Mabel to eat from her hand.

Five to wag her tail.

And seven to find the window seat.

It wasn't really a seat, not in the traditional sense. Just an old wooden bench with a cushion she'd re-stuffed years ago, tucked beneath the large front window that faced the street.

It had always been Edie's favorite spot.

A place to sip tea, knit a few rows, and watch the world shuffle by.

Mabel discovered it one morning after breakfast. Climbed up slowly, her back legs trembling a little, and settled onto the cushion with a sigh.

She fit there like she'd always belonged.

And from that day on, they watched the world together.

They never needed to speak much.

Sometimes Edie would narrate what they saw, "There goes Mr. Pearson and that ridiculous green umbrella," or, "Look, Mabel, the blue jay's back today." But mostly they sat in companionable silence.

They watched the mail truck pause at each house. The teenagers walk home from school with headphones in and heads down. The leaves change color, fall, and then return again in brighter green.

Seasons shifted softly while they stayed still.

On warm days, Edie would open the window just a crack. Mabel's nose would twitch at every breeze, catching the scent of grass, far-off grills, or the faint perfume of a neighbor's roses.

Sometimes people waved.

Sometimes they didn't notice the watchers behind the glass at all.

That was fine with Edie.

She liked the quiet rituals.

The two mugs of tea each day, one poured and one imagined. The crossword at 11. The bird feeder she refilled with trembling hands while Mabel waited patiently at the door.

And the window. Always the window.

Their lookout. Their shared pause. Their still point in a moving world.

One winter morning, Edie awoke to snow.

It blanketed the porch, softened the sharp edges of the hedges, and turned the view outside into something dreamlike.

She shuffled down the hallway in her slippers, heart already pulling toward the window seat.

Mabel was there before her.

She must've come down early, nudged the curtain aside with her nose, and climbed up on her own.

Edie smiled.

"Well," she said, wrapping herself in a shawl and settling beside her, "you beat me to it."

They sat like that for a long while, watching flakes dance in the streetlight.

No need for words.

Their breaths matched.

So did their silences.

Mabel had bad days sometimes.

Old bones, a weak heart, a bit of stiffness that never fully left.

Edie knew the signs. She herself moved slower, slept longer, and sometimes forgot where she'd put her glasses—even when they were on her head.

But they adjusted.

There were ramps added to the steps. A softer bed placed under the window. And when Mabel couldn't jump up anymore, Edie began lifting her, one arm under her belly, the other behind her chest.

"You and me, old girl," she'd whisper with each lift. "Window or bust."

They'd settle in, legs pressed together, and the world outside would continue its slow ballet.

Spring came. Then summer. Then another fall.

Some days were harder. Some were lovely.

Edie no longer thought in terms of years or numbers.

Just mornings. Just moments.

And however many Mabel had left—weeks or months or something more—Edie knew where they'd be.

At the window.

Always at the window.

Still watching.

Still loving.

Still there.

Together.

Chapter 12

The Moonlight Check-In

Lena didn't need an alarm or a calendar to remember when it was time.

At 10:03 p.m. every evening, like clockwork, Poppy would appear in the doorway. No bark, no fanfare. Just the soft tap of paws on the hardwood floor and a quiet presence by Lena's chair.

It was time for the moonlight check-in.

Lena closed her book and reached down, brushing her fingers through the dog's soft fur. Poppy leaned in gently, as if to say, *I'm ready when you are.*

"Alright, girl," Lena said, rising slowly. "Let's go see what the sky's got for us tonight."

They moved together, Lena wrapping her shawl around her shoulders, Poppy trotting ahead to nudge open the screen door. Outside, the air was cool and still. The back porch creaked under their steps, familiar as breath.

This had become their nightly ritual in the months after Bill passed.

It had started unintentionally, just a single step onto the porch one sleepless night when the house felt too quiet and the grief too loud. She had opened the door for air and found Poppy already there, waiting, tail wagging once as if she had known Lena needed company.

That night, they sat in silence under a thin moon.

And they had done it every night since.

The moon didn't always show up. Some nights, clouds blanketed the sky. Some nights it rained. But they still came out. Still sat side by side on the porch swing, the wood gently rocking beneath them.

Poppy would settle on the rug beside her, ears alert, gaze sweeping the yard.

Lena didn't talk every time. But sometimes, she did.

"I used to hate nights," she told Poppy once, months ago, when the porch light flickered and the stars were unusually bright.

"They got too quiet too fast after Bill died. I never noticed how many sounds belong to two people moving around in a house."

Poppy had shifted closer, resting her chin on Lena's foot.

"And when the kids left, well. That was its own kind of silence."

Her children, grown and busy, scattered across the country now. Ellie in Boston, Marcus in Portland. They called. They texted. But it wasn't the same as hearing their voices float down the hallway or seeing their shoes by the door.

Poppy didn't answer, of course. But she listened. In the way dogs do, with full body stillness and eyes that made you feel like someone understood.

So Lena kept talking.

In spring, they watched the tulips bloom beneath the porch railing. In summer, they listened to cicadas and the far-off bark of a neighbor's dog. In fall, the air turned crisp, and Lena began bringing out an extra blanket to drape over her knees.

One night in early October, she spotted a shooting star and nudged Poppy excitedly.

"You saw that, right?"

Poppy stood, tail wagging, and licked her knuckle.

It wasn't just a porch anymore.

It was their spot.

Their peace.

A place between past and present, where time slowed and breathing got easier.

That night, as Lena sat under a half-moon, she felt the usual calm settle over her shoulders.

She looked down at Poppy, who had curled beside the potted rosemary plant like always.

"You're a good listener," Lena said.

Poppy twitched one ear.

"And very punctual."

Lena smiled to herself, then leaned back and looked up at the sky.

"I think I needed this more than I realized."

She didn't say what "this" meant.

But Poppy knew.

It was a Thursday when things went off track.

Lena had spent most of the afternoon on the phone, first with the insurance company, then the doctor's office, then a long, circuitous call with Marcus that left her feeling more tired than comforted.

He meant well, of course. They both did. Her kids. They always asked how she was doing, always told her to "call anytime." But it wasn't the same as being here. And saying "I'm fine" over the phone never quite scratched the surface.

By the time dinner rolled around, she wasn't hungry. She made toast. Tea. Sat on the couch with a blanket over her legs and let the television flicker across the quiet room.

Poppy stayed close but didn't pester. She always seemed to know when to stay quiet.

When the clock hit 10:03, Lena didn't move.

Poppy did.

She stood at the edge of the living room, tail still, head tilted.

Lena looked at her.

"I'm just not up for it tonight."

Poppy stayed where she was.

Lena looked away.

She wasn't upset, not exactly. Just... low. The way some evenings pressed harder than others.

She stared at the TV for another few minutes, then stood up slowly and turned it off.

Poppy was still there. Waiting.

Without a word, Lena walked to the kitchen, poured the last of the tea into the sink, and pulled the shawl from the back of the chair.

"Alright," she said, softly. "We'll go."

The porch was darker than usual. No moon tonight. Just stars, scattered faintly above the pines.

Poppy took her usual spot by the rosemary. Lena sat down on the swing and pulled the blanket across her lap, her movements slower than usual.

They sat in silence.

A breeze drifted across the yard, tugging gently at the hem of Lena's sleeve.

She didn't speak, not for a long while.

Then: "I don't know what I'd do without you, Poppy."

The dog didn't move. Just blinked slowly, ears twitching toward a distant night sound.

"It's silly, but this..." Lena waved one hand at the sky, the porch, the swing beneath her. "This is the thing I look forward to most."

Her throat tightened unexpectedly. Not sadness, not quite.

More like gratitude, thick and quiet.

Poppy stood and walked over, pressing her head gently against Lena's knee.

"I know," Lena whispered. "I feel it, too."

The next night, Lena didn't wait for 10:03.

She was out on the porch by 9:50, the shawl already wrapped around her shoulders, a mug of chamomile tea steeping beside her.

Poppy padded out behind her and settled immediately beside the swing, as if relieved that the routine had righted itself.

Lena smiled, reached down, and scratched gently behind her ears.

"We're okay."

Poppy licked her hand.

And that was the end of it. No grand gestures. No big conversation.

Just a dog and a woman and a porch swing under the stars.

The check-in was complete.

A week later, the doorbell rang just after lunch.

Lena wiped her hands on a dish towel and headed to the front door, expecting a package or perhaps the neighbor.

But it was Ellie.

Standing on the porch, travel bag in hand, hair windswept from the taxi ride.

"Surprise," Ellie said, eyes crinkling. "I missed you."

Lena blinked. "But you—how—?"

"I moved that conference call to Zoom. I figured I'd rather work from your kitchen table than my shoebox apartment."

Lena didn't speak at first. She just opened her arms and let Ellie step into them.

Poppy danced in excited circles behind her, tail a blur of welcome.

That evening, Lena made soup. Ellie sliced bread and dropped cheese cubes into a little dish "for nibbling." The house, for the first time in weeks, buzzed with gentle movement: the sound of drawers opening, dishes clinking, laughter tucked into the corners of sentences.

Poppy seemed pleased to have another human to herd.

She followed Ellie from room to room, tail thumping each time Ellie looked her way.

"You're still doing the porch thing?" Ellie asked as she set two mugs of tea on the counter.

"Every night," Lena said, smiling. "Same time. She reminds me if I forget."

They stepped onto the porch at 10:03, as always. But this time, Lena didn't bring one mug—she brought two.

Ellie looked at the stars.

"Still as quiet as I remember."

"Quieter, sometimes," Lena said. "But not lonely."

Poppy lay between them, chin resting on Lena's foot, one ear cocked.

They sat in silence for a long time, just listening.

Then Ellie spoke, voice soft. "I always worried about you, out here alone."

"I know," Lena said.

"But now I think... I get it. The space. The pace."

Lena smiled. "And the company."

Poppy shifted, pressing closer.

"I didn't plan on her being such a... constant," Lena said. "But she is."

Ellie nodded, pulling the blanket tighter around her shoulders.

"I used to think check-ins meant phone calls or calendars. But I think they can be... this. Just showing up. Being still."

Lena reached out, placed her hand gently on Ellie's.

"That's all most of us need."

Ellie stayed three days.

On her last night, the moon was bright enough to light the porch in silver.

Lena and Ellie sat side by side, mugs in hand, Poppy stretched between them like a bridge.

No one said much.

They didn't need to.

The check-in had already happened.

And the ritual held.

Bonus Story: The Heart Behind This Book

Hi, it's Molly.

Before we close for the night, I want to share something a little more personal.

Most of the stories in *Paws & Peace* were inspired by other people. Friends. Readers. Strangers who told me about the small, meaningful ways their dogs showed up for them during different seasons of life. The stories are fictional, but the heart behind them—the ritual of a morning stretch, the comfort of a warm snore, the quiet companionship at the end of a long day— those are real. They came from conversations. From memories people shared with me that stayed long after.

But this final story isn't borrowed.

It's mine.

And it's the reason this book exists at all.

For a long time, I only had one dog. Just one. And to be honest, I liked it that way. She was my girl, my shadow, my sounding board, my everything. We understood each other. She knew my moods better than I did. She'd tilt her head when I talked to her like she was actually considering my point of view. She made life better, just by being in the room.

I didn't want a second dog. I liked my life the way it was. I didn't feel like I needed more.

And then, the pandemic happened.

Our world slowed to a halt. The playdates stopped. The visits with friends ceased. The long walks became shorter, quieter. She still wagged her tail when I looked at her, still leaned against me when I sat on the couch, but something had shifted. She was bored. And I was too, but I think I didn't notice it as much until I saw it in her.

That's when my sister stepped in.

She sent me a photo. No context. Just a text that said: "LOOK AT HIM."

It was a Chihuahua puppy.

Now, let me just say, I've always loved small dogs. Always. Even as a kid, I dreamed of having a little dog I could carry in my arms, one with big eyes, soft paws, and a tail that wagged every time I walked into the room. I never wanted a big, bouncy dog that could knock you over with excitement. I wanted the kind you could curl up with, the kind that could sit on your lap and even fit in your purse. Something fluffy, sweet, and endlessly snuggly.

My first dog was exactly that. A Bichon Shih Tzu mix, twelve pounds of pure cuteness. People called dogs like her "teddy bears," and she lived up to it completely. She had soft white curls, big soulful eyes, and the gentlest little face. She was affectionate and calm, playful without being chaotic. She'd trot beside me like we were in sync. She had this old-soul energy, like she understood things no one else did. And she carried herself like royalty. She was the queen, ruling the house and my heart, and she knew it.

So yes, I absolutely loved small dogs.

But a *Chihuahua?* That was never on the list.

You hear all the things, right? That they're barky, shaky, overly dramatic. Tiny tyrants with big attitudes. I'd never had one, and I wasn't looking to change that. I just couldn't picture it, a Chihuahua in my space, bouncing around and yapping at everything. I figured if I ever got a second dog, it would be another fluffy, easygoing companion like my first, not a crazy, ankle-biting maniac no one wanted to dog-sit.

But then there was that picture.

He was black and brown, with white paws and the tiniest tan eyebrows that made him look constantly concerned about the state of the world. His oversized ears flopped down like he hadn't grown into them yet, completely down, not perked up like I always imagined a Chihuahua's would be. In fact, nothing about him looked like what I thought a Chihuahua should be.

He looked like he could be an Instagram puppy, the kind that's so cute it almost doesn't seem real. His paws were comically small. His little belly was round and soft, like he'd just had a bottle and was ready to fall asleep in someone's lap. And his eyes—those shiny, serious, tender eyes—looked directly into the camera like he already had things to say.

He was so small. And soooo *ridiculously* cute.

Something inside me softened.

I still tried to resist. Told myself it wasn't the right time. Told my sister I didn't need a second dog. Told her he probably wouldn't be a good fit.

But I kept opening that photo. Kept looking at his little face.

And my sister, persistent as ever, knew just how to tip the scales.

She followed up with, "You should take him," my sister wrote. "Your girl is lonely. It's honestly cruel not to give her a friend."

Cruel. She went straight for the guilt.

"She just lies around all day now," she said. "No one to play with. You *know* she needs a buddy."

I pushed back. Reminded her I'd just been laid off, that one dog was plenty, and I didn't need to complicate my life any further, especially when I had no idea what I'd be doing next.

"You're being selfish," she said, only half-joking. "She's bored out of her mind and you *know* it."

Looking back, I'm not even sure she believed half the things she was saying. Maybe part of her did. Maybe she saw something I wasn't ready to admit, that my girl had grown quieter since the lockdowns, that she missed the energy of other dogs and people.

But I think a bigger part of her just really wanted someone to adopt that puppy.

And she knew she couldn't. Her husband had always said no to pets. It was one of those non-negotiables in their marriage. He wasn't a dog person, and she'd made peace with it, or said she had.

But when she saw that photo, something shifted. She didn't say it out loud, not exactly, but I could tell. I could feel it in the way she texted me five more times that night. In the way she called me after I didn't reply fast enough.

"I'm just saying," she said, "if you don't take him, someone else will. And it'll probably be someone who doesn't deserve him. Like, I don't know, a guy who leaves him outside all day. Or feeds him cheap food. Or gives him a dumb name like Buddy."

I laughed in spite of myself. "You're being dramatic."

"I'm being *realistic*," she said. "He's meant for you."

I told her I'd think about it. She knew that meant yes... even if I really was undecided.

She didn't let up. The next morning, she texted again. "You *need* this dog. He's your dog. He's just waiting for you to figure it out."

"I already *have* a dog," I replied.

"Yes, and she's lonely. And you're lonely. And I know you. You're going to keep thinking about him. You're going to keep opening that picture. Just do it already."

And the thing is... she wasn't wrong.

And I think she knew that. I think she knew exactly what she was doing. Not because she wanted to manipulate me, but because she knew me better than almost anyone else did. She knew where the soft spots were. She knew how to push in just the right way. And maybe she knew I needed that nudge, even if I didn't know it yet.

So that night, we were on the phone again, watching the series *You* together on Netflix, like we had been doing during those long, quiet lockdown evenings. The little boy came on screen, and we both lit up. We both loved Paco.

"Ugh," she said, "I love Paco. That kid breaks my heart."

I nodded. "He's the only character I actually worry about."

And then, casually, like she'd just thought of it: "That would be a great name for your puppy."

I laughed. "Paco? For a Chihuahua?"

"Come on," she said. "It's *perfect*."

And, of course... it was.

So I said yes. Quietly. A little reluctantly. But also with the kind of hesitant hope you don't want to admit you're feeling. I called the number. Arranged pickup. And a few days later, I met him.

He was smaller than I expected, even after seeing the photos. Barely three pounds, he fit in the palm of my hand. His whole body trembled, but his eyes locked on mine with this wild, intense focus, as if to say, *I'm not sure about you yet, but I'm here.*

I brought him home and held my breath.

My girl met him at the door, tail high, curious but cautious. She sniffed him once. He gave one small, ridiculous bark, somewhere between a squeak and a whimper, and then flopped onto his side like he had just run a marathon.

She licked his head.

And just like that, they were bonded.

From the very first moment, they were just... together. Like he'd always been there. She treated him like he was hers, no hesitation, no adjustment period. She slowed her pace to match his. Let him steal her toys. Gave up her bed without complaint. Even shared her favorite sun patch by the window. It was like she'd been waiting for him all along and just hadn't known it.

We were a pack now. A quirky one, maybe, a white fluffy girl with old-soul eyes, a tiny anxious pup with more energy than sense, and me, somewhere in the middle, trying to keep up. But somehow, it worked.

Paco was everything you'd expect from a Chihuahua.

He barked at the mailman, the neighbors, and the wind. He growled at dust bunnies inside and actual bunnies outside. He had opinions about which side of the bed was his. And as for the toys? Well, they were all his now, no question about it.

But for all his bossy little habits, he was fiercely loyal and endlessly cuddly, the kind of dog who would follow me from room to room and curl himself into my arms like he belonged there. Paco had woven himself into every corner of my days. I honestly don't know what I'd do without him. Life now feels so far from the moment I first saw his puppy picture, back before everything changed.

Both my sister and my first dog are no longer with me. One lost to a tragic car accident, the other to unexpected heart failure. The shape of my life shifted in ways I could never have prepared for, and there were stretches of time when I wasn't sure how to move forward.

But through the hardest time in my life, Paco was my constant. He was the one who got me out of bed on the mornings when I didn't want to face the day, and truthfully, if it hadn't been for him, there are days I might not have gotten out of bed at all. In a time when everything felt heavy and gray, he was the only sliver of joy, the one who filled the too-still evenings with his cuddles, his watchful eyes, his stubborn little presence. He didn't erase the grief, but he made it livable. One walk. One meal. One day at a time.

Time passed, and slowly, the edges of loss softened. The ache didn't vanish, but I could carry it without feeling crushed. And somewhere in that quiet space between remembering and moving forward, my heart opened just enough to imagine... more.

That's when I saw her. Zoe. All black, with four tiny white paws like she was wearing the softest little socks. The shelter staff said she was timid, slow to trust, but when I bent down, she pressed her head into my hand like she'd been waiting for me.

Bringing her home felt different this time. When Paco arrived, I still had my sister. I still had my first girl. This time, it was just me and Paco, both of us knowing, in our own ways, what it means to lose the ones who shaped us.

When Zoe first walked through the door, Paco didn't greet her the way my first dog had greeted him all those years ago. There was no instant bond, no effortless acceptance. He watched her closely, kept a little distance, and made sure she knew which toys were his. She, in turn, eyed him warily, unsure of her place.

But over time—day by day, meal by meal, walk by walk—they began to soften toward each other. Paco let her share the sun spot. She followed him into the yard. They learned the quiet rhythm of living side by side. And somewhere along the way, the hesitation faded. What began as tolerance grew into a gentle companionship.

It wasn't about replacing what was gone, it was about adding to what remained.

Paco carried me through the hardest season of my life. Zoe will walk with me through the next. And together, we'll keep carrying the love of the ones who aren't here.

This book is for them. And for every dog who has been more than "just a dog." The ones who keep us going when everything else feels too heavy. The ones who greet us at the door like we've been gone for years, even if it's only been minutes. The ones who listen without judgment, who notice when we're not ourselves, and who somehow know when to nudge us toward the sunshine. The ones who remind us that peace isn't found in the absence of loss—it's found in the presence of love, warm and steady, right beside you on the couch, in bed, or wherever life happens to find you.

Because in the end, it's never just about the years we have with them, it's about the way they change us, and the way they stay with us long after their pawprints have faded from the floor... but never from our hearts.

Closing

Thank you for spending these quiet moments here.

Whether you read one story at a time or a few in a row, I hope each one brought a little warmth, love, and stillness into your world.

These stories were written as gentle reminders that even in a world that moves too fast, there's beauty in slowing down, in showing up, and in simply sharing life with a dog who stays close.

Maybe there's a dog snoring at the foot of your bed... or one who follows you from room to room like your favorite shadow... or maybe one who nudges your hand when it's time to pause and rest. However they love you, I hope it feels like peace.

Because sometimes, that's all it takes to sleep a little easier:

A loyal heart.

A quiet space.

And the comfort of knowing it's okay to just be, with your dog and with yourself.

Sleep well.

Good night.